DIESEL
The Mavericks, Book 13

Dale Mayer

DIESEL: THE MAVERICKS, BOOK 13
Beverly Dale Mayer
Valley Publishing Ltd.

ISBN-13: 978-1-773364-14-8
Print Edition

Books in This Series:

Kerrick, Book 1

Griffin, Book 2

Jax, Book 3

Beau, Book 4

Asher, Book 5

Ryker, Book 6

Miles, Book 7

Nico, Book 8

Keane, Book 9

Lennox, Book 10

Gavin, Book 11

Shane, Book 12

Diesel, Book 13

Jerricho, Book 14

Killian, Book 15

Hatch, Book 16

Corbin, Book 17

Aiden, Book 18

Boxed Sets and Bundles

https://geni.us/Bundlepage

About This Book

What happens when the very men—trained to make the hard decisions—come up against the rules and regulations that hold them back from doing what needs to be done? They either stay and work within the constraints given to them or they walk away. Only now, for a select few, they have another option:

The Mavericks. A covert black ops team that steps up and break all the rules … but gets the job done.

Welcome to a new military romance series by *USA Today* best-selling author Dale Mayer. A series where you meet new friends and just might get to meet old ones too in this raw and compelling look at the men who keep us safe every day from the darkness where they operate—and live—in the shadows … until someone special helps them step into the light.

Traveling to China to retrieve a kidnapped scientist shows Diesel the depths of human depravity. Not that he needs more proof. He's been doing this type of work for a decade. This is the first time though the person he was rescuing was this interesting.

Eva Langston had been kidnapped while walking across the street and then locked up in a lab half a world away. Joining two other scientists, both letting her know there was no escape, she refuses to give up hope. When the rescue does come, it wasn't smooth or easy.

Still she was damn glad to be free. Until she realizes that

freedom is a long way off, as, one by one, her science team is picked off, leaving her the last one to be dealt with.

Sign up to be notified of all Dale's releases here!
https://geni.us/DaleNews

PROLOGUE

DIESEL EDWARDS WALKED back into his small apartment, even as his cell phone rang inside. He quickly picked it up and answered. It was Shane. "Hey, I was just outside, washing the car."

"And you didn't have your phone on you?"

"No," he said. "Sometimes I just don't want to be connected."

"Got it," he said.

"How are you two getting along?"

"Well, Shelly's back here in California, and we're looking for apartments right now," he said. "She's looking for a job but not pushing it."

"I wouldn't push it either. Her last job was a bit of a killer."

At that, Shane snorted. "You think? They did give her a nice severance package though, hoping that they wouldn't get sued for the lack of security. But, all in all, we're doing great."

"Perfect," he said.

"What about you?" Shane asked.

"Yeah, I'm back, normal, recovered," he said. "I had a few days of rest."

"That's good."

"Just a check-up call?"

"Well, I would invite you over for a barbecue," he said, "but …"

"But?" Diesel walked to the small balcony and stepped out. He was just on the outskirts of San Diego, and the smog was not too bad today, but it was pretty muggy. "So, you got a job for me or what?"

"Well, it's not me who's got a job for you. The Mavericks do."

"My own job?" Diesel asked in surprise.

"Yeah, if you're up for it."

"Any reason I wouldn't be?"

"I'm not sure," he said. "How do you feel about scientists?"

"No different than any other person. Why?"

"Because a specialist, an epidemiologist, has been kidnapped."

"And that's a Mavericks issue, why?"

"She was working on a new cure for a virus. Apparently China is looking to have the cure for themselves, and she is their best bet."

"Is it part of that H1N1 that's terrorizing Asia?"

"It's one of the offshoots of it," he said. "Anyway, she went missing twelve days ago."

"Why are we getting called in so late?"

"Because her family didn't report her missing."

"What family would that be?"

"Her brother, who lives with her. When he finally did call it in, nobody really believed him because he was drunk."

"Great, so how believable is her disappearance?"

"We checked the street cams, and two Asian males clearly escorted her, as soon as she left her home, into a black car."

"And?"

"It went to the Chinese Consulate. However, the consulate says nobody arrived."

"Did you show them the video?"

"Yes, but they say the car isn't theirs, and honestly the camera doesn't go clear onto their property."

"So what are the chances that she was even taken by the Chinese?" he asked. "It's pretty easy to blame them by taking her to that location but then sneak her off somewhere else."

"Yes, it's quite possible," he said, "which is why you're being called in for it."

"And what's the problem?"

"Well, I think at the moment she's on a Chinese warship."

"How did we go from the Chinese Consulate *not* having anything to do with her kidnapping to finding her on a Chinese warship?"

"Well, it gets better than that," he said. "Her last sighting was on a Chinese junk boat."

"Where?"

"Off China's coast."

"That's not making any sense."

"Nope, we'll fill you in as you go," Shane said cheerfully.

"Go where?"

"To the last sighting of her. How are your language skills? Like Chinese, possibly Vietnamese?"

"Terrible," he said. "I suck at it, but things always work out." As they spoke, he was already pulling out a duffel bag and packing up his clothes. He heard a vehicle outside and shook his head. "Are you telling me that that I'm leaving right now?"

"Aren't you packed yet? You should have started when I

first called."

"I might have, if we hadn't been talking about you guys and a barbecue that you owe me," he said. Nonetheless he was packed within minutes.

"Make sure you've got your passport."

"I've got it," he said. "I still don't understand why this scientist was kidnapped."

"Well, she's got a scientific background for one. She's a renowned epidemiologist for another, and she's got some head start on a cure for this … this virus."

"That's great, but then somebody wants her for a lab, right?"

"Well, that's what we're hoping for, but, of course, it could just as easily be extortion."

"And we don't know."

"Well, that's for you to find out," he said. "In the meantime, we're still tracking her movements. Please bring her home." And, with that, Shane went to hang up.

"Wait," Diesel said. "When am I leaving?"

"I thought I made it clear that you're supposed to be packing."

"Not only am I packed, I've locked up my apartment, and I'm standing outside."

"Oh, well, do you see the little red car parked in front of you?"

He looked at the parking lot and found it. There appeared to be no driver. "Yeah?"

"The keys are under the floor mat."

"Where am I going?"

"Head to the Coronado base. You'll take a bit of a convoluted route."

"Why is that?"

"Because the Chinese government says they don't know anything about it, yet they're obviously involved. So we're staying under the radar."

"Hey, that's … We've still got to get there fast."

"Yep. Don't worry. You'll get there fast. Your flight's leaving in about forty minutes. Make sure you're on it."

And, with a laugh, he hung up, leaving Diesel to hop into the little red Mustang and to hurtle toward the airport on the base. He didn't know whose car this was, but it was a hell of a way to leave town.

And, with that thought uppermost in his mind, he hit the gas and went forward to whatever life would bring.

CHAPTER 1

DIESEL EDWARDS STOOD on the surface of the destroyer and watched the land approach.

When Shane had said Diesel would be flying really fast, Shane had meant it. Diesel hadn't quite expected his flight to be this fast, but he'd taken a base flight and was even now sitting on the destroyer, as they came upon the Chinese coast. The Chinese government wasn't happy to have them as close as they were and had put out their own navy ships.

"Where to from here?" he muttered to himself. He pulled out his phone and the material he had on file. Eva Langston was still missing, and nobody had seen any further signs of her.

The latest intel found her disembarking the junk boat onto a vehicle traced to a lab just outside of a major Chinese port city. After that, she disappeared.

He figured she had been moved into some secret Chinese government lab, where they hadn't let her out, so her face would not be picked up by facial recognition off any street cams or satellites. Diesel would go to the last-known location and see what he could find.

As he stood here on the destroyer, someone spoke from behind him.

He turned in surprise and watched as Jerricho Hickory walked toward him. "Jerricho?" He reached out a hand and shook the other man's hand.

With red hair and a bright grin and enough freckles across his cheekbones to make him look like a fourteen-year-old, Jerricho was every bit the big capable seaman Diesel knew well. Besides, at six-two and two hundred pounds of lean mean fighting machine, no one could mistake Jerricho for an adolescent anymore. "What are you doing here?"

"Well, I might say that a Maverick called me."

At that, Diesel's eyebrows shot up. "Shit, really?"

Jerricho gave him a lopsided grin. "Yeah, really," he said. "I just arrived. I saw a ship come in on the other side. I wasn't exactly sure what that was about."

"I landed on the other destroyer," Diesel said, "but I'm here now."

"I think we're taking off soon too," he said, as he turned to look back at the helicopters getting ready.

"Yeah, I hear that as well," he said. "I'm ready to go." He looked at him and asked, "How's your Chinese?"

"Not bad," he said. "How's yours?"

Diesel winced. "Actually I suck."

"Maybe that's why they asked me to join in for this one?"

"Maybe, I'm glad to have you here regardless. Been a long time."

"Well, let's go see what kind of damage we can do." Just then a shout came behind Diesel. He raised a hand in acknowledgment, turned, and snatched his duffel bag. He looked at Jerricho. "You ready?"

"Always," he said, "you have to be in this business."

"Isn't that the truth," he said.

The two raced over and boarded the Black Hawk helicopter that would take them closer to their target location.

This US Black Hawk supposedly looked like the Chinese version. Diesel hoped so, for the safety of them all. It would be a short trip, which helped them too. As soon as they landed, the two disembarked and disappeared into the streets.

"That was pretty easy," Jerricho said. "If we had landed and had to report to somebody, that would have taken us forever."

"Definitely an advantage of this new system," he said. "We report to nobody."

"I like it," Jerricho said.

"I mean, that's why the *Mavericks* name," he said. "None of us are particularly good at following authoritarian orders anymore."

"I follow the orders that make sense," Jerricho said, "but lately it just seems like some of the brass aren't making any sense at all."

"If they don't have boots on the ground or haven't had in a long time," Diesel said, "it's pretty hard to accept some of the stuff that they tell us to do. I wasn't quite ready to quit, but I was thinking about it when I was approached."

"Same here. I was trying to figure out what came next. I'm not sure that this is even the answer as much as, right now, this is what's next," he said. "I did hear talk about bigger jobs with the whole teams."

"I think there are bigger jobs with multiple members. These are all smaller jobs with two men," Diesel said. "But, if we need more manpower, of course, more men are available. The issue is that sometimes you need six or eight guys to do a job."

"Got it," he said. "And I'd be okay with that, as long as I respected the guys I was with."

"And that's always the answer," Diesel said. "The last thing we want is to have somebody we don't trust on the team when we're out on a mission. And, if we haven't worked with them for a long time, it's pretty hard to find trust for them."

"Exactly."

They disappeared into the sights and sounds of the city.

"I don't even know why Shanghai was chosen," he murmured. "I would have thought the kidnappers were somebody other than the Chinese government. You know? Like, maybe to say another country did the kidnapping and then maybe took her here, if that was the original plan," Diesel said.

"But it's a little too obvious that China's involved."

"Meaning that somebody is trying to make it look like China?"

"Well, China is the easy bad guy, isn't it?" Jerricho said.

"True enough." Diesel thought about it for a moment and then said, "Well, we have to figure out who's behind it for the scientist to be safe after her rescue. But, at the same time, I don't think that's today's issue as much as it is finding her."

"Maybe, but then we also have to make sure that we can get her safely away, and that might require finding out just who is behind all this."

He nodded. "Suggestions?"

"I'm not sure how the information flows among the Mavericks, but we need intel, and we need it now."

"Not only do we need intel," he said, "we need some weapons."

"That I can arrange," Jerricho said with a grin.

"Legally?"

"Are you asking for that?"

"Hell no," he said. "I just need to have what I need to have."

"So give me a list of what you want," Jerricho said.

"I can do that, as soon as I stop walking long enough to write it down for you."

They headed toward their hotel and arrived shortly. They quickly registered, moved upstairs, and, once inside, searched for bugs. They tried not to take too long about anything, knowing that their progress would have been watched throughout the city. And Diesel sat down with a pen and paper and quickly jotted down what he thought they would need. Then he ripped off the page, handed it to Jerricho, and asked, "How's that?"

"Perfect timing," he said, looking at his watch. "We're almost at the dinner hour."

"Right. I haven't eaten. How about you?"

"I'll place an order for this stuff," Jerricho said, lifting the list. "And I can pick up food at the same time, if you want."

"Perfect," Diesel said. "I'll start ordering intel."

"You didn't already?"

"I did and got a lot of it, but you've got me thinking more about who's behind it," Diesel said. "So let's see what else we can come up with."

And, with that, Jerricho walked out of the hotel room.

Diesel logged into the Mavericks chat box, while he thought about Jerricho's connections and how this might be very helpful in the job. And then how the hell did the Mavericks know about his connections? Diesel grabbed his encrypted cell and pressed a Speed Dial button. As soon as Shane came on the line, Diesel asked, "How did you guys know about Jerricho?"

"He's been on the radar for a while," he said.

"Makes sense, I guess. He seems to be the right person for here."

"His stepmother is from China," he said. "She took over his care when he was really little. So he's fluent in their languages, and he's been to China, particularly that area, for many years."

"Well, his expertise will be welcomed," he said. "Otherwise I'd be skulking through the shadows."

"Skulking through the shadows is what we do best," Shane said.

"That's the truth," he said. "I'm wondering about something that Jerricho brought up, as to who's behind this. If it were the Chinese, wouldn't they have used another party to kidnap her?"

"They're getting bolder, and they're getting a little more aggressive with that *thumbing their nose* attitude," Shane said, "so I wouldn't count that out at the moment. It took a lot to dig down and to find her current location—a random sighting at a Chinese harbor as she was moved onto land. We didn't have a solid confirmation at the time, but we do now."

"Okay," he said. "I want all plans for the area, where she disappeared or was last seen. I believe several commercial buildings are in that area. What does the actual underground network here look like?"

"I'll find out what I can," he said, "but check out this first."

And, with that, Diesel heard a chime and clicked the link he had in chat and was taken into the street views of Eva Langston's home in Boston. It took him a moment, and then he saw her walk to her car. Another vehicle drove up, blocking hers. There wasn't even a visible struggle. And the vehicle suddenly left, and she was no longer in view. "That's the SUV that the Chinese Consulate denies was theirs, right? Even though they drove there, I understand."

"We presume the Chinese used third-parties, so they could deny this initially. We tracked all their transport transfers, which were many, and most recently found her in Shanghai. See here." Shane dropped another link, showing another black vehicle turn a corner into what looked like a huge commercial parking area.

"Near our hotel, I presume. And was that vehicle traced?"

"It was, and it was stolen."

"Of course it was," he muttered. "And who can park there?"

"Only those who work at this series of warehouses."

"But it would be easy enough to steal a parking spot too."

"Yes, and we find no other camera feeds showing her in or out."

"It'd be too obvious that she's in there though," he said.

"Depends if they thought anybody would notice. The other thing is, she could have been moved out at any point in time further down the road," Shane said.

"Yes. Any reason to suspect she's in danger?"

"Not as long as she's cooperative."

"What's her temperament like?"

"She lives for her science. She would not keep quiet about being pulled away from her projects, her research."

"There could have been some consolation that she would continue to work."

"Maybe," Shane said. "She's also a rebel, who doesn't take kindly to authority, and only plays the game so she can get grant money."

"Interesting. And her father?"

"He's another big-name scientist, but he's also very much an animal activist," he said. "So she's been raised with that similar attitude."

"I guess," Diesel said, "the question is, when we find her, if she would help in her rescue or if she will be a hindrance, and I'm better off to knock her out."

"I would definitely give her at least a chance to let you know the answer to that on her own," Shane said with a note of humor.

"I'll give her at least three seconds," he said. "First sign of trouble and she's out."

"She's known to be very resourceful," he said.

"So then the question is, is she doing anything to help herself?"

"When you find her, you can ask her yourself."

"Got it," he said.

As soon as he checked out the various related links, he brought up the additional history on Eva. A fair bit was in here. She lived a quiet life after her father was arrested for some activism, where he'd been arguing local politics. He'd taken his daughter on several of those trips. When he was arrested, it had been a traumatic experience for her, and she had stayed home more or less ever after and then had devoted her adult life to scientific research, rather than public protest.

Diesel could understand that. Especially as a child, that would have been rough.

On the other hand, she'd created a medical breakthrough, and mankind was desperate for it. She'd been working on a number of diseases from the basic building blocks of the malaria-carrying mosquitoes that started it all. And now she was working on something a little more definitive. He didn't quite understand all this part, and it certainly wasn't a disease currently emblazoning the world, but she had an awful lot of research that had somehow made a breakthrough with stem cells.

He wondered if it wouldn't have been easier to just grab her research instead of taking her, depending on how well she was known to be a difficult person.

As he read through more, he learned she was single, had no children, had no living mother, was supporting her adult brother with known addictions. That would also be difficult for her as well. And since her father had retired and had moved away, she was left with nobody in Boston to defend her when she ran into trouble. Neither was anybody looking after her.

Frowning at that, he thought about what her life was like as a single person on her own, taking care of her alcoholic brother, trying to save the world from global diseases with no known cure to date. That couldn't have been easy. At least the brother was living in a group home at the moment so that had to be easier on her.

When a knock came on the hotel door, he froze. But he got up, slowly walked to the side, and, as he got there, the door opened in front of him.

EVA LANGSTON TOOK a long slow deep breath, studied the keyboard in front of her, even as she watched the guard walk behind the three different scientists. He was busy talking on his phone—yelling into his phone was a better description. The other two scientists, another woman and a man, looked at Eva and frowned. She nodded and kept her fingers moving on the keyboard. They had to show some results, or else it would turn out very badly. It was important to keep their heads down and to make it look like they were compliant, working. They were guarded every minute of every day. The guards switched out every eight hours, and they had a guard at nighttime. They were given food, time on their own in their rooms, but they had no electronic devices in their rooms. No way to call out for help, no way to do anything, and all their time on the lab computers was almost always monitored.

A team of security guards on the other side of the lab's observation window watched them, even as this particular gunman walked back and forth, yelling into his phone.

She didn't know how much longer she could do this. The strain was showing. One scientist had committed suicide. She wasn't even sure how he'd done it but presumably had found a way. At least he committed suicide according to the guards. It was a reminder that their livelihood was dependent on the guards' goodwill.

She didn't know who was behind this, but they were in China, so it wasn't hard to guess. But it was easy to blame the Chinese government, and she had no way of knowing if that were the case or not. But she'd heard enough horror stories of some of the things going on over here to make her blood curdle. Including the fact that the resistance and other religious groups opposing China had been plowed underground and were used to harvest organs for transplants for the Chinese citizens who could order up what they needed.

It was a scary thought, and one that made her blood run cold. If that were the case, that's what their end would be as well.

Unless she could get the hell out of here.

She had no clue how to do that, and she had nobody in Boston who would call in the alarm or give a crap. Although she had a decent job, it was still just a job. And, if she didn't show up one day, a few might cry about it for several minutes, but her five minutes of fame would quickly die out. And they had her research, so it's not as if they would care about her personally.

She had had some major breakthroughs on the work that she was doing, but that didn't mean that anybody there couldn't just carry on with her research. That's also the problem here; they had provided her with copies of a lot of her own research, which didn't make her happy because it had been put in the wrong hands. Although she was a firm believer that, if her findings healed anybody, then they were in the right hands. But, if it were to hurt anybody, then it was in the wrong hands, and that seriously sucked.

She wanted her work to help people, not be weaponized into a global disease to be utilized against chosen civilizations. She kept working and then pulled her hands off the keyboard and rubbed her eyes.

"Are you okay?" Marge asked, beside her.

Eva smiled and nodded.

But the guard snapped, "No talking."

Marge immediately turned her head back to her keyboard. Neither of the women handled any of this very well, and Paul, on the far side, was even worse. He just glared at the guard, and the guy raised his rifle, as if to hit him in the head with the butt.

"She just asked if I was okay," Eva said immediately.

He again glared at her and said, "No talking."

She sighed and turned back to the keyboard. It was hard to do what she needed to do when they didn't have the same lab setup. She had told him that she needed certain equipment, and they hadn't gotten it for her yet. Apparently it was coming, but, in the meantime, she was writing up her reports as best she could. But what she really wanted was to get the hell out of here.

She checked the timing, knowing that the guards would change out in the next two minutes. And, sure enough, just like clockwork, there they went. She smiled at that and relaxed a little bit, as she watched the smaller man come in. The dude was not really abusive, like the other one, who just seemed to enjoy pushing his power around.

Eva felt the other two scientists relaxing slightly as well. But this replacement guard was a little more agitated today. He told them, "No talking," then walked to the security guards in the observation room next door, had a conversation with them, and then returned to the lab, where she and the other two were working.

"Make sure," he said, in a ringing voice, "that you do not have anything to do with any strangers who have just arrived in the country."

She looked at him in surprise. "Sorry?"

He glared. "They are coming to rescue you. If you leave with them, we find you, and we kill you," he said succinctly.

She blinked several times. "We don't even know what you're talking about."

He nodded. "Good." At that, he turned and walked away.

But inside, hope flared. Was somebody actually coming

to look for them? How would the Chinese even know? Did that mean they were watching all the airports to see who came and went? That would mean that this rescuer was somebody well-known to China. Was that even possible? Did they keep track of every anti-terrorist group out of the US? Surely they couldn't do that. But then, thinking about the technology out there—once the faces, names, physical descriptions were input—it wouldn't be all that hard to keep track of people. And that was a sobering thought.

This guard walked to the far side, on his phone as well, playing games, it seemed.

Marge beside her asked, "Does that mean somebody's looking for us?"

"I don't know," she said in an equally low tone. "I wouldn't count on it."

Marge's shoulders sagged.

"But we could get lucky," Eva murmured, hating to see the older woman lose hope.

Marge nodded. "Anything would be better than this," she whispered. She reached up a shaky hand to brush the gray tendrils of hair off her face.

"I'm sorry," Eva said. "You've been here longer than I have."

"Too long," she said, "way too long."

Eva thought Paul had mentioned how Marge had been here for about six months—Paul even longer—but Eva couldn't be sure. She knew that the woman was suffering from her captivity regardless. The time didn't matter; it was all about the effects of the time on someone under these adverse conditions. It was hurting Marge in a big way, and that would be hard. Eva nodded and smiled. "Keep strong," she said.

"Don't know if I can," Marge said very softly. "It's tough."

"It is. I'm sorry," she whispered.

"You're younger," Marge said. "I'm almost done."

"Don't talk like that," Eva said, her voice a little sharper than she intended.

Instantly the guard raced back over. He reached out and pummeled her shoulder with the rifle.

Almost immediately her arm went numb. She winced, holding back the cry, as her arm fell from the keyboard, and she lurched forward.

"I said, no talking."

"No," she said, "if I can't talk, then I can't work, and, if I can't work, then I'm no good here."

"Then we kill you," he snapped.

"Then kill me," she said. "If you keep hurting this arm, I can't work anyway."

He just glared at it, hanging limp by her side, backed up a little bit, and said, "Stop talking."

She rubbed her sore shoulder, while she pulled on whatever little bit of reserves she had. Marge was right. It was hard to stay positive when you had been through this day after day after day. And the longer it went on, the more that victim mentality overcame you. Eva needed to stand strong.

Because the mental strain was the worst.

Just as she checked her watch, she realized it was almost time for the day to end. They worked in the lab ten to twelve hours, but today they'd started late. So she didn't know if they would be forced to stay late too.

A knock came on the door, and immediately the gunman was there, his rifle ready. The door was opened, and two businessmen stood there and snapped out orders in

Chinese. Immediately the gunman raced toward the scientists, held up the rifle, and told them, "Stand up. Stand up. Stand up."

CHAPTER 2

E VA STOOD UP immediately, her hands in the air.

The three of them were led out of the lab and immediately taken back to their rooms.

Not a sound was made as they followed obediently along. There were other white doors, potentially other labs; she didn't know for sure.

There might have been other kidnap victims too, but again she didn't know.

When she was back in her room, the door was locked, and she was left alone. She sagged down on the single cot and buried her face in her hands, wondering how long this would be. How long before the world found out, and, even if it did, did anybody give a shit? The last thing she wanted was to be here until she was old and gray. She figured that she'd end up with a bullet before then anyway because they weren't the easiest to get along with.

As it was, she sat quietly in her room, and a tiny rap came on her wall, and Eva knew it was Marge. It was the equivalent of holding hands. She rapped back ever-so-softly. And, of course, Marge didn't rap again. Eva just guessed that Marge would have laid down and relaxed now.

Eva flopped back down on the bed and crossed her arms over her chest. She didn't even know how to put out a warning. She had no window in her room, no way to contact the outside world.

Apart from the little knock between her and Marge's rooms, there was no communication at all. Paul was also here, on the other side of Marge.

Until her food was delivered, this would be her world. She had a small bathroom, where she could shower and use the facilities, but that was it. She had a ten-by-eight-foot space, where she tried to do some exercises, tried to walk and pace, but it was pretty hard to do in such a small space. Mentally she needed it though. And, with that in mind, she slid upright in bed, crossed her legs, and worked on her yoga. If nothing else she needed to cut her stress. Because her heart and mind were just screaming at her. What had just happened with the strangers expected here, and was there any hope that someone was coming to rescue her and the others?

DIESEL STEPPED BACK, behind the door, as it opened up.

When nobody entered, a man called out, "It's me."

Diesel sighed and stepped forward and said, "You should have given me a warning." But seeing him, he realized why he didn't. His arms were full. "What the hell?" he said, as he opened the door wider to let Jerricho in.

He quickly dumped his armloads on the bed. Then, in his hand, underneath everything, was a bag. He handed that over to Diesel and said, "Takeout."

Diesel brought it to the table and quickly emptied the food. "All this?"

"When I placed the munitions order, I decided to get everything at the same time," he said, "so this is what you asked for."

He stared at Jerricho and then at the bed. Immediately he walked over and opened up several cases. One was a box with grenades, the other contained C-4 and ammo, and they had nice little techno goodies. He stared at Jerricho, surprised. "That was fast."

"Yeah, it's fast. It was a cash deal, and, of course, I suspect he tried to follow me. After all, this is a lot of weapons here. Plus, he's curious and greedy. I had to try to lose him. I highly suggest that, after we eat, we change rooms."

"I'm up for that. I suggest we change hotels," Diesel said.

"Even better."

The two men sat down, quickly scoffed down the food, hardly even tasting it. And yet street food was some of the best food in the world, as far as Diesel was concerned.

By the time they had emptied their plates, Diesel quickly packed up the little bit that he had, and, taking half of the gear that Jerricho had brought back with him, the two men slipped from the room and locked up. They even took the food containers with them to ensure nothing was left for DNA tests.

As soon as they reached the back street, Jerricho asked, "Where to?"

"I sent Gavin and Shane a message," Diesel said. "We're a block up and around the corner."

"Perfect," he said.

They quickly made it into the front entrance, which led into a dark shadowy hallway.

Diesel's phone buzzed. He pulled it out and said, "Room 157. First floor at the far back."

"Perfect."

Diesel and Jerricho headed down the hallway to their

room and found it empty and open. They quickly stepped inside and shut the door. Diesel kept his phone line open, putting it on Speaker now. They unloaded everything onto the two beds. This time he put the firearms together and quickly loaded then. He filled his pockets with spare ammo and asked, "Do we have a location?"

Shane answered this time. "We have movement," he said. "Sending you a link."

As Diesel opened up the link, a group of twelve well-armed men left their SUVs and entered an industrial building beside where their vehicles were parked—within walking distance from either hotel where Diesel and Jerricho had been.

"What the hell are they after?" Jerricho asked.

"I'm hoping they're on protective guard duty," Diesel said quietly. "Were we made? Are they moving Eva? Or worse?"

"It's possible we were made but not necessarily by the Chinese," Shane said. "Our sensors also picked up several Russian spies."

"Oh, don't tell me that they're after her too?" Diesel asked.

"They might not only be after her," Shane said, "but it's quite possible they're buying her." With that, Shane ended the call.

"Shit," Diesel said as he pocketed his phone. "That doesn't sound healthy either way."

"Who the hell is she?" Jerricho asked.

"A scientist with some stem-cell research on germs and viruses, and I think maybe they're looking at it for germ warfare. So a cure for their country and a killer for the rest?"

"Does anything surprise you anymore?" Jerricho said,

staring at Diesel.

Diesel shook his head. "No," he said. "I'm continuously amazed at the absolute depravity of humanity against humanity." He sighed. "Let's hope that's not what this is all about."

"Regardless," Jerricho said, "we have to figure out how to get into that building."

"Well, getting in would not be a problem, but, depending on what firepower we find inside, getting out will be."

"We saw a dozen go in."

"But people will be inside too."

"So at least fourteen. We have to find a way to flush them out," Jerricho said.

"Now that's a good idea," Diesel said, looking at him. "What do you have in mind?"

"Gas?" he said immediately.

Diesel thought through the ramifications and asked, "Do we have enough gas masks to get her out?"

"If we plan to take her up through fresh air, it would be easier," he admitted.

"No guarantee there's any fresh air close by."

"We also have to consider the difficulties of us getting in and out with the added gas element too."

"Well, obviously we'll need to be masked," Diesel said.

"I know, but I was wondering about the guards."

"Well, we can take them down with the gas, which will make them a lot easier. But what if more captives are there, not just Eva?"

At that, Jerricho winced. "Right, and, of course, you'll want to save everyone, won't you?" he said with a note of humor.

"Won't you?" Diesel challenged.

"If I can, yes. You know tough decisions are likely to be made on something like this."

"I know," Diesel said. "That doesn't make it any easier."

"No, not at all. But … let's take a look at the ventilation shafts," he said.

As soon as they were set up in the new hotel, with everything available in front of them, Diesel and Jerricho went through the HVAC system online to see just what was available for pathways.

"We could probably put something in through here," Diesel said, pointing, "but no guarantee that the air vents go all the way through."

"If the gas doesn't reach the prisoners, that would be just fine by me," Jerricho said. "One person to carry is one thing. Carrying two or three? That'll be an impossibility."

"I know," Diesel murmured. He studied the ventilation system and said, "I think we can do it. We come through this side."

"And, even if we do," Jerricho said, "what's our exit strategy?"

The two now held the blueprints for the lab building itself in front of them.

And then Diesel saw it. "This set of windows on the first floor is near the ventilation shaft here. And a second-story balcony is above, which might come in handy."

"But we don't know where the prisoners are."

"We'll have to go room by room for that."

"Which is dangerous and slow."

"But we don't have any better intel," Diesel said. He studied the blueprints again and said, "If it were me, being the nice guy that I am, I'd give them all rooms with windows and fresh air to keep my prisoners healthy, but these kidnappers won't care. Likely, if these scientists can't do the job, they'll shoot them and dispose of their bodies anyway. So why waste a better room and the chance of them being visible? Eva is probably in a basement, where they have no ventilation."

"Which just means they'll get sicker, weaker, all due to the poor living conditions. Keeps their prisoners docile."

"Hell, they could be using the damn viruses on them," Diesel muttered.

Jerricho looked at him. "Remember. We'll think positively about humanity."

"Yeah, let me know how that works out for you," Diesel said.

Jerricho snorted at that. "Unfortunately we've seen too much of the other side of life."

"I know," he said, "but there's always hope."

With rudimentary plans in place and a message sent off to Shane, telling the Mavericks what their plan was, the two suited up and slipped out into the night. With full backpacks and carrying the bag full of the rest of their needed gear, they moved quickly to the building in question. They checked for video cameras and hadn't seen anything other than the street cams, but that didn't mean something else wasn't here. That was always a problem. They had to make their approach stealthily and as quietly as possible and avoid those street cams. And they needed to take out as many people as they possibly could.

With Shane running intel in the background, they moved ahead to the car park, where the vehicles were, and into the entrance where the twelve men had entered.

He whispered to Jerricho, "I wish we knew if any of the twelve had exited."

"We didn't see anything on the cameras," he said.

"No, and now we've disabled the cameras, so we can get in, but how long before somebody realizes they are down?"

"Hard to say," he said, "but I wouldn't give it much time. I suspect they're already expecting some movement. But why would the Chinese deal with the Russians?"

"It depends whether it's for or against them."

"Meaning that, either they're here for the scientists or they're trying to take them?"

"Maybe one of their own was kidnapped as well," Diesel said.

"Wouldn't it be nice if we actually had help with this?" he said. "We could have, you know, a joint effort between the two countries."

"Well, let it be different countries than these," he said with half a smile.

"Sometimes they're okay," Jerricho said.

The darkness was absolute. Mother Nature was being kind to them tonight with heavy cloud cover. The moon was up there somewhere, but not even a slice of it was visible in the sky. They headed for the door, and, just as he was about to enter, Diesel immediately grabbed Jerricho and pointed out a broken window off to the side. The two exchanged grim looks and nodded. Slipping inside via the window— and hoping against hope that the twelve who entered earlier weren't only here to kidnap the same people—the two men entered the building and moved slowly forward.

They had the gas with them, and that was still the plan, but now, seeing that broken window here, all of a sudden gave rise to the possibility that some other enemy faction was in play. The men moved a little more slowly and a little more quietly. Something was going on that they couldn't see, and they needed to know what it was before they got caught in the same damn trap.

As they headed forward, they heard voices down one hallway to their side. They immediately slipped to the corner and stayed quiet. It was a dialect Diesel didn't understand. He looked at Jerricho, who shook his head. Therefore, it wasn't Chinese.

Great. So what did that mean?

But the voices were low, stealthy. Diesel poked his head around a corner to see them, heading to the far side of the building. He looked at Jerricho and motioned behind him that they take the other hallway. They would need night goggles at this rate. They had brought night vision goggles with them but hadn't thought the inside of the building would be quite so dark. The fact that this other team was here gave rise to them having already put things into motion that Diesel and Jerricho weren't expecting.

Pulling out their goggles, they quickly adjusted the plan on the fly. They needed one prisoner and only that one prisoner. If these other guys were taking somebody else, that was fine.

Diesel just hoped that they were taking them because they were allowed to take them. And, if these guys were to kidnap these scientists for just another lab, he wasn't down for that either. But, as the dozen men appeared to have come up from the one hallway, and they were still looking for whatever, then Diesel and Jerricho had a chance to get there before them.

Moving swiftly, they checked down another parallel hallway and went downstairs. Diesel would bet that nobody would waste a good room upstairs, where the scientists could be seen, if there was room downstairs. The other team headed down their hallway, and he presumed up. Diesel moved with silent precision through his hallway to the stairwell and smoothly moved downstairs, Jerricho in tandem. With their night goggle visions, they didn't need anything else.

They moved through the hallways like ghosts, looking for prey, both enemy and friendly. As they headed down another hallway, he heard a sound. He quickly ducked and bolted behind a corner to have two men walk in front of him, both carrying weapons, both talking in rapid Chinese. He looked back at Jerricho, and jointly they slipped out, grabbed both men, and took them down.

Taking the two dead bodies in the corner, looking for a place to stash them, Diesel found a closet on the far side.

With that found, Diesel dragged his man inside, as did Jerricho, quickly disarmed the men for weapons that they might need themselves, and moved out into the hallway again.

Jerricho said, "You know that we could question one of these guys next time."

"With this other team moving in here, we have to take speed and stealth as the prime objectives."

"Oh, I agree, but, if we had a chance to talk to one of them, we could possibly get answers."

"We'll get some answers," he said, "just not enough." At that, he motioned for Jerricho to lead, as they slipped down the hallway where the two gunmen had come from. They made it through two side rooms, checking inside both, and they were empty. But they were small, self-contained, and looked very promising in terms of housing prisoners.

When they got to the third one, they heard voices inside. Both of them stood back on either side of the door, and the voices got louder as whoever was inside came out. Diesel couldn't understand the dialect, but he had his phone out, a translation app working, trying to discern what was going on. He trusted that Jerricho was catching the drift.

As soon as the door opened, another two men stepped out, and one was still talking. And it was just as easy to take down both of them at the same time. He looked at Jerricho to see his guy was dead too. He checked inside the room, saw it was empty, apart from what looked like a small fridge and a table. Probably their lunch room or meeting room. They dragged both men back inside and stuffed them in the far corner. From there, they stepped out, once again heavily rearmed, and he looked at Jerricho as they walked forward. "Did you learn anything?"

"No, they were talking about a sports game."

"Of course," he said, "they are just men after all."

"I know," he said. "It would be nice if they had answers to this whole mess, but it never happens that way."

As they moved forward, they heard gunfire somewhere else in the building.

"Shit," Diesel said.

They moved forward to the next door. It was locked.

He rattled the door and heard a woman's voice call out, "Who's there?"

"Who are you?" he asked in English.

"I'm Eva," she said. "I was kidnapped from the US in Boston."

"Well, Eva, you're the one we came for," Diesel said. "Stand back, please."

Immediately he kicked the door down and entered, rifle at the ready. But she was alone, sitting on a bed, curled up in the corner. He quickly held up his flashlight, checked her over, checked the room, and then held the flashlight up against his face, so she saw him. "My name is Diesel Edwards," he said. "Come on."

"Wait," she said. "Did you get the other two?"

"Which two?" Diesel asked. She motioned at the wall adjoining the next room down the hallway. Jerricho immediately moved to it. "Are any of them Russian?"

"No, I don't think so," she said in confusion. "Our kidnappers are Chinese."

"Yes, another team's in here," he said, moving her toward the door.

"Another team helping you?"

"No," he said, "they're against us."

"That makes no sense," she said in confusion.

"I know. Are you hurt, or is there any reason you can't run?"

"No, I'm not hurt. Getting tired and a little weak from the lack of decent food and the stress," she said, "but I'm okay."

"And the other two?"

"They're also okay. Their names are Marge and Paul."

"Good." At that, Diesel turned, and Jerricho had opened the next door, and a woman, Marge he presumed, stood there, shivering.

Immediately Eva raced over and wrapped her arms around her. "They're American," she said. "They're here to rescue us."

Marge just nodded, but her expression looked a little confused.

Diesel asked, "Where's the third one?" They both pointed to the next door. Diesel raced over, kicked the door down, and brought out the third scientist.

"What's going on here?" Paul asked in a flat voice, as if he'd seen too much and had no hope anything good was happening.

"Do you have any connections to the Russians?" Jerricho asked instantly.

Paul looked at him, surprised, and shook his head. "No," he said, "I've been here so long that I don't even know what's going on anymore."

Diesel checked his watch, sent a text message to Shane on his phone, and turned to look at the three of them. "We weren't prepared for three of you."

"There were a lot more," Eva said quietly. "They didn't make it."

"Any of them Russian?"

"Yes," Paul said. "What is this about Russians though?"

"Another team is here, not with us, but they're going through each of the floors—trying to find you guys, we presume. We don't know because, of course, we haven't stopped to ask them."

"Oh, my God," Paul said. "We need to get out of here."

"What do you know about the Russian captive?"

"He died," Paul said. "He was not all that healthy to begin with, and we're down here without sunlight, and we work seven days a week without a break, and we're not fed properly. He was getting weaker and weaker. I know he thought he had sent out an alert, requesting help, but nobody came, and he got very depressed."

"Well, the help looks like it came," he said.

"But too damn late," Paul said, with a plaintive cry.

"Why are you even here now?" Marge asked.

"We got word about Eva," he said. "We didn't know about you two."

"I am American, but I've been working out of Australia," Marge said.

"I'm American too," Paul said, "but I was over in Switzerland."

"You were just plucked from your various labs?" Jerricho asked.

"Yes, that's a good way to put it," Paul said. "I've been here over a year. I've seen two others, and one was here for a few days and then disappeared."

"Any idea why?"

He shook his head. "I never saw him again."

"Well, we'll get this information going forward," he said. "Right now I want you two to stick close. And, if you have any injuries or health conditions, you need to tell us. We can't carry three of you."

"I'm fine," Eva said, her voice stronger. "I haven't been here as long as they have been."

"No," Marge said, "but you keep getting bashed because you don't listen."

"I don't take well to authority," she said slowly. "Besides, it was you they were trying to hurt."

Marge, the older one, looked at her and smiled. "I told you that I probably wouldn't make it through this anyway."

"And that's no reason to give up." Eva turned to look at Diesel. "Can we leave now?"

He had his phone in his hand. "I'm trying to track where the Russians are. We don't want to meet them."

"Somebody needs to tell them their comrade died a while back," Paul said in disgust. "It would have done him a lot of good if they could have been here in time."

"I don't imagine arranging something like this is all that easy, plus just finding us," Eva protested.

"That's the reason we found you. Eva was picked up on a street camera."

"Oh," she said in delight. "I deliberately kept my face up, facing forward, hoping that somebody would find me."

"Yes, facial recognition caught you," he said. "So good job." He looked at the young woman and smiled. "You actually look a little familiar."

"No idea why," she said, "unless you are interested in talks on stem cell rejuvenation virus for virus multiplication."

"Well, I think everybody is probably interested in it, but I can't say I've ever attended any lectures like that," he muttered.

"No," she said, "not unless it's your thing."

"Well, I'm not sure what my thing would be outside of the fact that this is the work I do," he said, ushering them toward the stairs. He said to Jerricho, "I don't like the idea of going back out the same way."

"We'll take the balcony."

"And what do you think the chances are that we've got the Russians here?"

"I'm not sure," he said, "but we have to make a decision, and we've got to follow through."

Up ahead they heard more gunfire. Immediately the captors cried out and clustered close. He motioned at Jerricho. "Let's take this hallway off to the side. Sounds like the Russians are finding some targets. I don't want our group to be next."

"Out the back?"

"No, that's most likely the place they'll come looking," he said, "but we have to stay away from the gunfire."

"Jesus, yes," Eva said, "please stay away from the gunfire."

Ushering the three out, they asked them as many questions as they could about the layout. "We've seen it on blueprints," Diesel said. "Do you have any thoughts that you can add as to where the men, the armed guards stay, how many there are, things like that?"

"Well, something's definitely up," Eva said. "The guards started acting more difficult today. And instead of us staying in the lab all day, we were moved from the lab abruptly and locked in our rooms."

"The Russians were found. Caught going through the airport today," Diesel said quietly.

"So then the Chinese should be expecting the attack today," Eva said.

"Maybe. Did they double the guards?"

"They did," she said. "We've had four on us all the time."

He looked at Jerricho and nodded. "We've taken out four," he said.

The scientists just looked at him mutely.

"What we don't know is how many others could be here. We have video of a dozen Russians coming in."

"Great," Paul said. "So we're still heavily outnumbered."

"Maybe," Diesel said. "Let's keep moving."

Racing as fast as they could, they headed down the hallway toward the back. At the service elevator, he stopped, pushed a button, and then stepped back out, as it went upward. He took the stairs down, motioning for them to join him.

"What was that for?" Eva asked.

"A decoy," he muttered.

"Won't that send them down here?" Eva asked.

"But we won't be here," he said.

She just shrugged and kept on going. "As long as you know what you're doing," she muttered.

"I don't think you trust very easily, do you?"

"I do," she said, "but I also like to see some proof. So, if you tell me that it's this or that, then I want to know that this is the truth, and I have something that visually allows me to confirm it."

"Life isn't always so clean-cut," he warned.

"It's never clean-cut," she said. "That's why I like science. When you work with it, it's black-and-white and easy to understand. But all this theoretical stuff drives me crazy."

"Not everything is theoretical though," he said.

"I know. I know that," she said, "and sometimes I wish it was a whole lot better than what it is."

"Got it," he murmured. "In this case, it's concrete enough that we will move with it," he said. "But we can't take any chances of getting caught, so, as soon as there's any kind of firepower going on, you need to drop to the ground and stay down there."

She nodded slowly. "If you have a spare gun," she said, "I can shoot."

He looked at her and smiled.

"Really, I can."

"What? Are you from Texas?"

"No, Wisconsin, but I used to go hunting with my father."

"That's a surprise," he murmured in a low voice.

"I hated the killing part," she said, "but my father wanted to make sure that, when push came to shove, I could do the job."

He nodded slowly and said, "Well, I do have a spare rifle, so I might take you up on that."

She looked at him, looked at the weapon on his back, and said, "I'll take it right now actually." And she quickly disengaged it from his shoulder and put it over hers.

He shrugged and said, "If I see that you can't handle it …"

"Got it. If I can't handle it, you'll take it away from me."

"Exactly."

She shrugged. "It is what it is. I just don't want to feel like a victim anymore."

"Understood. Were you taken from work?"

"At home actually." She sighed. "Who'd have thought that we weren't even safe in or near our own homes? Since word of my work got out, my life became even more public."

He said, "I imagine that would have been hard."

"Very much," she murmured.

As they moved ahead, Marge turned to look back, saw the rifle now in Eva's hand, and gasped. "What are you doing with that?" she asked.

"I don't want to be taken by any of these assholes again," Eva said in a hard tone. "This is my insurance that I won't be."

CHAPTER 3

EVA ACTUALLY HAD another reason for wanting the gun, and that was more because of her own fears. Her mother had been shot in a break-in when Eva was just seven. She'd heard it happen, and it's the reason why her father had made sure that she knew how to handle herself, if she were ever in a similar situation. She couldn't help back then, as the gunman had come in, fully weaponized himself, and hadn't given anybody any chance.

He'd been high on drugs and shot up her mother, leaving her bleeding on the kitchen floor, while he grabbed food. Eva had called 9-1-1 and stayed hidden upstairs. She watched him leave out a window, and, as soon as he had disappeared, the officers arrived. She'd raced downstairs to help her mother, but it was too late. She told the officers where the gunman had gone, and he'd been picked up not very long afterward.

But her father had come home, his grief over the loss of his wife overshadowed by his anger, realizing that his traumatized daughter had been left alone in the house during the murder and could easily have been killed herself. After that, he'd taken it upon himself to help her learn more about self-defense and to ensure that she wasn't quite so easily taken.

Regardless, when the men kidnapped her from her home

some twelve days ago, they pulled a gun on her. She knew the odds of fighting armed men. However, she certainly knew how to use the weapon with her right now, and it gave her a little bit more confidence. She understood that the professionals would say it was false confidence and that she certainly shouldn't count on it.

Often in these home invasion scenarios, it was common for the gunman to take the weapon from the homeowner because they weren't sure that they wanted to shoot somebody. But most of these gunmen forcefully entering a house did not care one way or the other if they did kill someone. Same as with these gunmen in the Chinese lab.

So Eva had learned a big lesson. Twice now. When you raised a firearm, you had to be sure that you were ready to pull the trigger.

Right now she was more than ready to pull the trigger. She also knew that poor Marge and Paul couldn't handle too much more. She whispered to Diesel at her side, "Marge seems quite ill, and Paul has not been feeling well for the last few days."

"Anything serious?"

"Despair is possibly one reason. Marge won't talk about what may be ailing her. As scientists, we have a tendency to know a little more about our symptoms," she said. "So I wouldn't be at all surprised if they have a good idea but just aren't sharing it."

He nodded. "Any reason to think they can't keep moving like this?"

"They definitely can't for the long-term. Can they keep up some pace? Yes. I just don't know how long or how fast."

"We have to get out of the building," he said. "After that, it's a whole different ball game."

She nodded.

Up ahead was more gunfire. Jerricho turned, sent a hand signal to Diesel, who then took the other two scientists and headed left.

Diesel took Eva right.

"No," she said, "we don't want to do that. We need to stay together."

"We have to," he said.

"Why?" she asked.

"Because we've got a Russian team of a dozen agents coming ahead. Too many of us to hide in one place."

"What if we can't take them out?" she muttered. She stared around her, struggling to see in the dark. She generally had great night vision, but this was a whole different story. It was complete blackness all around. "Don't suppose you have more night goggles, do you?"

"No," he said. But he wrapped something around her waist.

"What's that?"

"It's a rope," he said. "When I say I want you to stay close, I mean it."

She gasped as he tied the other end around himself. "Isn't this actually worse?"

"It's a weird darkness in here," he said.

"I think they were doing experiments with lights, altering infrareds, et cetera," she said. "I know I often thought the hallways were really weird. We're also still low in the ground."

"We've actually come up one full flight of stairs," he said. "The lights can be very disorienting."

As they kept moving forward, she said, "You can't be there to help your friend, if he gets into trouble."

"No, I'm not," he said, "and he won't be there to help me, if I get into trouble."

She studied his shadowed profile, wondering at a life where he was prepared to step out into danger, without anybody to back him up. "You're really good at this, huh?"

"We all are," he said, "but we don't, in any way, delude ourselves into thinking that it's still not a fatal job."

"I'm sorry," she said. "I was thinking my job wasn't all that dangerous. Now I've changed my mind completely."

"The company you work for should have supplied security, once you made your breakthrough."

"I don't even know how anybody knew. I don't even know how much of a breakthrough it is. I haven't been able to do any testing," she said, knowing the frustration in her voice was obvious.

He gave a light laugh. "And I guess that's everything to you, isn't it?"

"Well, that's definitely a lot. This is my life's work."

"Got it," he murmured. "And that makes a huge difference."

"It really does. I just know that we're starting to have excellent treatment results on some of these viruses."

"Any in particular?"

"We've been working on several." She listed them, and he shook his head.

"Those are pretty major. The plague?"

"It still exists," she said, "unfortunately."

"I had no idea," he said.

"And it's still deadly," she said. "But because it doesn't show its head very often, we tend to think that it's been dealt with. But it's still there, and it's still in the US too."

"That's unbelievable," he murmured.

"And one of the things that I'm trying to deal with is some of these latent diseases."

"And the stem cells are doing it?"

"Yes," she said, "similar to the way that they're helping HIV patients. It boosts the immune system, so you can get the stem cells where you need them."

He nodded. "And is it the delivery system that you perfected or what? Because stem cells and stem cell research has been around for a while."

She laughed. "Yes," she said, "exactly that. It's a matter of taking the stem cells, making them do what we wanted them to do in the body."

"Got it," he said. "So you could pretty well cure anything?"

"I wouldn't go that far. We're really just at the beginning of that research." She felt her lungs starting to burn as they raced forward. "How much farther?" she gasped.

He looked around and said, "We're coming around the side to where Jerricho and the other two are, making sure that this is a clear pathway. We didn't think that the other two would make it as far."

"No," she said, "definitely not."

"Which is why you are with me," he said cheerfully.

"Great," she moaned. "I was afraid of that. I just realized that I should have said I was in just as bad shape as they were."

"But, you aren't," he said. "You're full of nervous energy and looking for a plan of action and frustrated because you can't get it."

She stared at him in surprise. "Wait. Are you a shrink?"

"No," he said, "not at all, but it's my job to understand the people I'm picking up because I need your cooperation to do what I need to do."

"You have it," she said, "just even being out of that damn room is a joy. Nothing like being locked up and knowing that nobody will give a damn about opening up your cage to let you out before you die."

He looked at her in surprise.

"That's one of those forever fears after being kidnapped and held captive like that," she murmured.

"Did you ever think that there was a time when they would just lock you up, walk off, and throw away the key?"

"Every day when they locked me in," she said flatly.

"I'm sorry," he said. "That's hard."

"Very."

"Well, the good news is, you're out of the room, and I don't intend on ever having you go back in again."

"But intentions aren't necessarily plans," she clarified.

And he chuckled softly. Then he immediately calmed his voice. "It's nice to see you have a sense of humor," he said. He held up his hand and stopped, and she realized they had come somewhat around in a circle.

"Are they up ahead?"

"They are, and they've also been taken," he said.

DIESEL PLACED A finger against her lips and said, "Don't speak again. Not until I say so." And he quickly moved forward, giving her no choice but to follow, since they were still tied together. He heard the Chinese words firing rapidly up ahead and heard Jerricho respond.

He looked at her and whispered, "Do you understand Chinese?"

She shook her head.

So far, Jerricho was being treated with respect, so he must have said something, but Diesel didn't have a clue what. His gear would have given him away if nothing else. But just one male was up against Jerricho and the two scientists with him.

As Diesel watched and waited, the lone man lifted his rifle and held it against Jerricho.

Diesel immediately drew his weapon, and, before the guy could fire, Diesel popped him.

Jerricho looked at him and asked, "What took you so long?"

"I was trying to figure out what was going on," he said. "Anybody else around here?"

"No, I took two more down."

"Good. Let's go," he said. He looked at the other two scientists. "Move it now."

Paul struggled to his feet, and Diesel frowned, studying his weakened condition.

"We'll head to the second floor, where there's a balcony," he said. "We've arranged to get out that way."

"Good," Paul said. "How far is it?"

"Directly above us," Diesel said, "so not very far." With that, he led them all back around up to the stairs. They cleared the hallway, moved across to the small sitting room, where the small balcony was, and stepped outside.

No alarms went off. No lights went on. No gunfire was heard.

He quickly dropped down the ropes, looked at Jerricho, and asked, "Do you want to go down, and we'll take the other two between us?"

He nodded. Jerricho slipped over the balcony with Paul

on one side and slowly lowered himself and Paul down.

Eva said, "I can go down on my own."

Diesel untied the rope from her and quickly wrapped it around Marge. Diesel nodded at Eva to go first. Eva slowly climbed down the rope, keeping it wrapped around one leg, down from knot to knot, until she reached the pavement. After that, he picked up Marge and told her, "Put your arms around my neck, and hang as tight as you can."

She nodded and buried her face against his neck, and he slowly lowered himself down with the older woman. When they hit the ground, Jerricho came up and helped him to release the hooks up above. They didn't want to leave anything to show their exit passage.

As soon as they were on the ground and clear, they tied up the ropes and Diesel threw them over his shoulder. Grabbing Eva's hand, he pulled her off to the side and whispered, "Stay close."

She nodded. "We are."

"I know, but what about those two?" He nodded in the direction of Paul and Marge. Diesel didn't say anything, but Paul still worried him.

As they moved forward, Paul stumbled once and then again. Jerricho bent down, helped the older man to his feet, and asked, "Are you okay?"

Paul shook his head. "I'll make it. I'll make it." But a desperate note was in his voice.

"You didn't expect to make it out of there, did you?" Diesel asked Paul.

Paul looked at him in surprise. "What do you mean?"

"Just something in your tone, something that's not quite what I expected."

Paul frowned at him. "How could I possibly have

thought I'd be saved? I've been a captive for a year," he said bitterly.

"I get it." But Diesel kept an eye on him. He glanced at Jerricho, frowned, and shook his head.

It was enough that Jerricho knew Diesel was disturbed.

As they moved forward ever-so-quietly, Diesel stopped short of a corner. As they came around the corner, Jerricho swept low and Diesel swept high, and then Paul stepped out. Seeing a vehicle, he raced forward. Then came a single shot, as Paul's head exploded, and he dropped to the pavement.

Jerricho immediately rolled behind another vehicle, and, all of a sudden, he stood, leaned over the trunk of the car, raised his rifle, and he fired off three shots. There was a groan and then silence, before a heavy *thud* was heard. Jerricho immediately raised his hand and motioned for his partner.

Diesel swept the two women forward into the back seat of the car, as Jerricho jumped into the driver's side, and Diesel too landed in the front seat.

"Is this your car?" Eva asked from behind them.

"No," Diesel said, with a grin. "Not sure whose getaway car it is at all."

"So how do you know it's safe?"

"We don't," he said cheerfully.

"Jesus," she muttered.

"You want to stay there and discuss it?" Jerricho asked her in surprise.

"No," she said. She looked at him and frowned. "Did you get him? The man who killed Paul?"

"I did."

"Good," Marge said passionately. "Paul didn't deserve that."

Diesel looked at Jerricho and shrugged.

"What do you mean by that?" Eva asked him.

"By what?"

"That look."

"Something was going on with Paul that I didn't understand," Diesel said.

"Like what?"

Diesel sighed and said, "It crossed my mind that he might have been a spy. He might have been making his life a little easier by tattling on whatever conversations you guys were having in the lab."

Eva just stared at him blankly.

Marge cried out, and then, in shock and anger, she said, "He wouldn't do that."

Diesel looked at Eva and asked, "Would he?"

She stared at him wordlessly, considering his question.

He nodded. "Think about how long he's been here. Think about what his future looked like. Think about what the hope of actually being released would do for him."

Eva nodded slowly. "Paul was very conflicted, and we never quite understood why."

"You can't surely believe him," Marge said, motioning at Diesel.

"I don't know what I believe," Eva said, turning to look at the older woman. "You know Paul better than I do."

"Of course I do," she said passionately, "and he wasn't the kind to do that."

Eva nodded. "And again, in your case, would you have done something like that?"

The older woman looked at her in horror.

"Think about it. If you were promised to get out of here in a couple days or a couple weeks, would you have reported on our conversations?"

Marge stared at her, and her shoulders slumped. "I would have," she admitted. "And honestly I would be very angry right now if that's what Paul had had for a deal, and he hadn't shared it."

"He couldn't have shared it," Eva said.

"I hope he didn't have that as a deal," she said, "because then that freedom was taken away from him as well."

"It's pretty hard not to think about a deal like this," Eva said to her.

"I really liked him," Marge whispered.

"So did I, and I certainly wouldn't judge him for trying to end this hell."

"No," Marge said, tears appearing in the corner of her eyes. "He was a good man. I refuse to believe anything different."

"You don't have to," she said gently. "Even if he did whatever he needed to do to get out of here, we can't hold that against him. You and I both know how terrible it was in there. And we haven't been here as long as Paul was."

Marge nodded slowly. "It was so awful." And she started to cry softly, her tears painful in the silence.

Jerricho turned to check the rearview and side mirrors.

"Are we being followed?" Diesel asked.

"No," he said, "nothing that I can see."

"What a mess," Eva said.

"Well, I wasn't expecting the Russians," Diesel said.

"We need to get the word out," Jerricho said.

Diesel pulled out his phone and sent Shane a message. **We are out plus 2. Gunfire in lab building. Probably Russians cleaning house. Need safe house.** He turned to Jerricho. "What do you want to tell him?"

"That the Russian kidnapped scientist died a couple weeks ago."

Diesel turned to Eva. "Do you know any of the details?"

She shook her head. "No, I don't." She looked at Marge, but she still sobbed in the corner.

"I've asked for a safe place for the night," Diesel said, quickly reading the answering text.

"Good," Jerricho said. "We need a place to rest, and I don't know if the women need medical attention."

Diesel looked at the other two. Eva shook her head, but then she nodded toward Marge. "Marge, are you okay physically?"

She looked up with tears washing her cheeks, still experiencing heavy sorrow. "I'm okay. If I can get out of here, I'll be that much better, and I will recover," she said a little more robustly. "It's just so very sad to think that something like this is allowed to happen."

"And, if you had a place to go home to, would you go back to Australia or home to the US?"

"Honestly right now, back to Australia, but I don't know if that's even feasible."

"We'll do what we can," he said. He looked at Eva. "You?"

"The US," she said, "Boston." He raised an eyebrow. She shrugged. "That's family."

"Got it," he said. At that, he sent off several more messages and waited for a response. While he waited, he checked the roads around them. "Still so empty."

"I know. It's like the calm before the storm."

"Don't say that," Eva said from behind them. "The last thing we want is any more attacks."

"Doesn't matter what we want," Diesel said. "Chances

are, it's in the works." There was silence behind him. He twisted, looked at Eva, and asked, "You okay?"

Fear was in her gaze, but she nodded slowly. "Does this ever end?"

"Yes," he said. "Are you working for a private company that'll sell your research?"

"Maybe," she said, "but I'm a contractor, and part of my stipulations for working with them was that a certain amount of my work would be allowed to go to the public for free."

"Well, if you did that in this case," he said, "nobody would have to kidnap you for your research, would they?"

"I don't know if the company went through with it."

"Or your kidnapping didn't give them a chance," he said.

"How many people have to die for this to be something that others can work on too? Monetizing these cures," she said, "that's where the big money is and where too many focus, instead of saving people."

"I get that. I still want to understand how these drugs cost what they do because it seems like it's ripping off the little guy at the end of the day. However, if you keep creating breakthroughs, then this problem may never go away."

"Great," she muttered.

"Or you make it part of your next contract where maybe you give your newfound drug cures to the poor for free. But, for sure, the company must be required to supply security."

"I hear you. I don't know what that would be like, after having guards at my back for the last ten days in that lab."

"No, and there's never an easy answer," he murmured.

"I get it. I just wish that we had a better system."

"Well, think about it," he said. "Come up with an idea that would make you happy over all this and present it to your company. And let's hope your company isn't involved in some way."

She winced at that. "I don't even like to hear you say that. I don't know why they would be. They are already in on my research."

"Right, but this breakthrough gives the company an awful lot of publicity now, doesn't it?"

"I hope not," she said, staring at him in shock.

"Why?"

"Something like this isn't ready for publicity."

"But didn't the stocks go up?" he asked in a dry, sarcastic voice.

She sagged back. "I don't think I like the way your mind works," she murmured.

"Maybe not," he said, "but it's usually the reality of things."

CHAPTER 4

EVA STILL REELED from the thought that Paul had been killed. It hurt to consider he might have turned against them. Did she blame him? No, she didn't because she hadn't been there very long, yet her captors had been horrible. To even consider this was a lifetime sentence, she probably would have grabbed at any opportunity to change it. But it hurt seeing Paul murdered like that and knowing how distraught Marge was. It was easy to see just how downhill everything was going right now.

Still Eva was damn grateful to be out of there. She couldn't imagine the endless anguish Paul must have faced, being stuck there in captivity for over a year.

As she sat here in the growing darkness, she wondered just where she would end up. She leaned forward and asked, "Is there any way to tell my father that I'm out?"

He looked at her in surprise. "Does he know you were kidnapped?"

"Probably not. He went underground after a big upset a while back," she said quietly. "He lives in a cabin out on one of the Wisconsin lakes. At least I hope he still does."

"Do you have a number for him?"

She nodded and gave it to him.

He quickly typed the number into his phone and called it.

When it rang continuously, she stared at it in surprise. But then a familiar voice came through the phone. "Hello."

She snatched the cell from Diesel's hand. "Dad?"

"Eva," her father shouted.

"Hi," she murmured.

"What are you calling for?"

And then she realized he had no clue. "I just wanted to hear your voice," she said, catching Diesel's look, as he shook his head.

"Well, I'm always happy to hear from you," he said. "Normally you don't sound this worried. Are you coming to visit soon?"

"You know what? I think I will," she said. "I don't exactly have a date just yet."

"That's fine. It's good to hear from you," he said.

"How is the fishing?" she asked, tears coming to her eyes. She wiped them back, trying to keep her voice clear, as the tears clogged her throat.

"It's perfect," he said. "The best decision I ever made was to move out here permanently. You should come and fish a bit."

"I think when I come that I'll stay for a few days."

"In that case, something's going on in your world," he said worriedly.

"No," she said, "I just realized I'm in need of a break."

"Great," he said, sounding relieved. "Let me know as soon as you can, and I'll set up some of the best fishing spots, and we can go out."

And she smiled because she knew that, for her dad, these days really meant spending all his time on the lake fishing. But that was okay too. "You got any new friends?"

"Maybe," he said, with a cheeky tone. "What about

you?"

She smiled, looked at Diesel, and he raised an eyebrow at her. "No, still single, Dad."

"You can't work all the time," he said gently. "There's more to life than that."

"I know," she said, "but I've lost an awful lot in life too."

"And you can't have your mother's death be what drives you."

She heard the grief in his voice. "If I'd done that," she said, "I would have gone into gun reform."

"I know you love her, but don't let this mark your entire world."

"Wouldn't that be nice?" she said. "Anyway I just wanted you to know that I love you."

"And I love you too," he said.

After ending the call, she gave the phone back to Diesel and whispered, "Thank you."

He nodded. "What happened to your mom?"

She winced. "A break-in. He entered and shot my mom in the kitchen to get some food," she said. "I was seven, upstairs, hiding in my room."

"Oh, my God," Marge said, beside her.

She nodded. "It's one of the reasons why the kidnapping was particularly difficult for me," she said. "I never really realized how much your history wraps around your psyche and hits you where it counts."

"Always," Diesel said. "But you seem to have worked through it."

"I don't know about that," she said softly. "As my father said, I've let it dominate a lot of my life. Took me a long time to stand being locked up—as I was in my closet, while it was going on."

"And, of course, you heard it all," he murmured.

She smiled weakly, nodded, and said, "Yes. I wanted to go into law enforcement for a long time and then realized that I really only wanted to put them in jail. I learned that the killer was high on drugs, and he was on drugs because his family had been decimated by disease. He couldn't handle the grief. That's when I decided that there was no point in treating the symptom. I needed to work on the cure."

He looked at her in surprise.

She smiled. "I know. Kind of an ideological way to go through life, but it worked for me. I found that scientific lab work was actually where my heart belongs, and so I've been really enjoying it," she said, "until now."

"Let's keep it that way."

"You're safe now," Jerricho said.

"Do you think so?" she said. "Or will we still be looking over our shoulders?"

Both men stayed silent at that.

She nodded. "Any chance of food?" she murmured. "We haven't eaten in a long time."

Jerricho nodded. "As soon as we can. We'll find a safe house first."

"Where?"

"That's the question," Diesel said. Just then his phone buzzed. He looked at the screen and said, "Now I have an address." He held it out for Jerricho, who said, "Pop that in the GPS, will you?" And, once in the GPS, they took a look and said, "We'll be there in ten minutes."

Jerricho quickly changed lanes, turned around corners, and headed in the right direction for their safe house.

She sat back. "Ten minutes? I can handle that." She looked over at Marge, smiled, patted her hand, and said,

"Smile, we're almost safe."

She nodded. "Maybe, but it's only an *almost*," she said.

"We're not locked up anymore."

Marge whispered, "Exactly."

Eva caught Diesel looking at Marge, curled up in the corner of the seat, her head against the seat back.

"I'd just like to be on US or Australian soil," she said, with a yawn.

"Food, a shower, and a good night's sleep," Eva said, "and everything looks different."

Marge smiled at her. "It'll look different, but it'll still look Chinese."

She laughed at that. "Well, that's fair, since we are still in China." She looked over at Diesel. "Thank you, by the way."

"You're welcome," he said with a smile.

"Is this what you really do for a living?" she asked, fascinated.

"Right now, yes."

She nodded and said, "It's just amazing."

"What?"

"That we're even alive," she said. "It's just hard to believe, at this point, that I was locked up in that small room, and now I'm here. It's like a dream. Or maybe more like waking up from a nightmare."

"Well, I'm pretty sure that you'll be locked up in a hotel room next," he said cheerfully.

She groaned. "Seriously?"

"Until we can get you back home again."

"At least it's progress." She stayed quiet, until they went through a series of turns at multiple corners, and she realized that their behavior was ever-so-slightly erratic, yet controlled. She leaned forward and asked, "Are we being followed?"

"We hope not," Jerricho, the driver, said, "but we can't take the chance."

And, just like that, they dipped into an underground parking lot and parked. She looked at him and said, "Now what?"

"We're here," Diesel said. He hopped out, opened the vehicle, and helped her out. Then he quickly removed the duffel bags that they had and some of the gear that they had taken off the guards. Keeping an eye on her and Marge, Diesel and Jerricho ushered the two women between them, as they led the way to a set of stairs, where they were quickly moved upstairs.

"Is this a hotel?" Eva asked.

"No," he said. "We have an apartment. A safe house."

But it was an apartment in a big building, so, as they moved through the hallways, she was surprised that nobody else appeared to be around, and then, just as suddenly, the guys had a door opened, and they were inside.

She took a step in and noted several bedrooms and a bathroom, all fully furnished. She turned to look at him, smiled, and said, "Now all we need is food."

"Not to worry, it's coming."

She nodded, walked over, and took the first bedroom, which had two twin beds. She dropped onto the closest one and closed her eyes.

"Are you sure you want to sleep?"

"No," she said, "not at all. Maybe a shower first but it just looked too inviting not to lie down."

"Maybe, yet the food's coming. So how about a quick shower and then food?"

She looked over at Marge, who was sitting on the edge of the second bed. "Marge, do you want a shower first?"

Marge shook her head. "No, I'll eat, then shower, and then sleep."

So Eva got up, looked at the guys, and said, "I guess you can't magically produce some clean clothes, can you?"

"I can have them for you by morning," he said.

She nodded and headed to the bathroom. She stripped out of her clothes, entered the warm flowing water, and scrubbed herself down, top to bottom. By the time she was done, she felt the weariness pulling on her. She put her uniform back on again, and, while busy braiding her hair into a long braid down her right shoulder, she stepped back out and headed for the kitchen.

There the smells hit her first.

"I didn't realize that it had arrived." She looked at the array in astonishment. "I didn't hear this arrive, and there's so much of it."

"Won't be for long," Marge said. Her plate was already heaped high.

It was noodles and who-only-knows what else, but she didn't care. Eva held out her empty plate, and Diesel pointed at the food and said, "Serve yourself."

She helped herself to a decent portion, then sat down. "I feel so much better after a shower," she said, "but it also made me more tired."

"To be expected," he said. "After eating, you can go to sleep."

"Good. I'm looking forward to it," she admitted. "As long as we're safe, then hopefully I'll sleep."

"We are right now. We'll run guard on four-hour watch-es,"

She stared at him. "And that implies that it's not safe then?"

"Safe enough," he said. "This is a precautionary measure."

"I hear you," she said, "but it doesn't sound very precautionary. It sounds proactive and defensive."

He just grinned and said, "Let us worry about that."

"I guess I will, since you've done well so far."

"Exactly," he said, "this is what we do. Remember that."

She nodded slowly and looked over at Marge. "How are you doing?"

"I'll be a lot better when I'm back on friendly soil, like I said before," she said. "But food is helping, not being in that damn lab is helping. And the fact that I know a shower is right around the corner and a comfy bed makes it even better."

"Right," Eva said, "the beds in that place were terrible."

"Just cots, I presume?" Diesel asked.

"Exactly, they didn't care about our comforts at all."

"No, and why would they?" he said quietly. "You were expendable."

She winced. "Do you really think they were looking at it from that point of view?"

"I would think so," he said. "Either you performed or you didn't, and they would get someone to replace you." He looked over at Marge. "How many captives did you see?"

"Several," she admitted. "Sometimes the guards told us what happened. Sometimes they didn't. The people were just there, and then they were gone."

"And then I arrived," Eva said.

"You were the latest, yes," Marge said, "but in no way is it done."

"Right." Eva nodded and continued to eat.

Marge quickly finished off hers and said, "I'll go have a

shower now." She got up and excused herself.

The men looked over at Eva. "Are the two of you okay?"

"We're fine. We've been through a lot together, but I was a relatively new acquisition for the captives," she said, "so I don't really know how much Paul and Marge have gone through themselves."

"Right." The guys didn't say anything more.

She smiled and said. "Are you worried about her?"

"Of course," Diesel said. "There are a lot of reasons to be worried. But the bottom line is, you're here now, and we'll do our best to get you back to the US safely."

She had to be happy with that.

DIESEL DIDN'T THINK Eva really understood how ill Marge was. She had probably made a point of not letting Eva know. It was also possible that Marge didn't know how ill she was, but there was a yellow tone to her skin. The whites of her eyes were not a healthy-looking white. And he'd seen what appeared to be a tumor on the back of the woman's underarm area. And one under her jawline, probably resting at the top of her throat. She needed medical attention. She needed it fast.

What he also didn't know was whether she had contracted whatever it was that was hurting her at the lab. Was it possible that the Chinese lab was actually utilizing these scientists as lab rats as well? That didn't bear thinking about. But, of course, his mind now didn't want to let it go. As he sat and waited for Eva to finish eating, appreciating the fact that Eva plowed through a decent amount of food, he said, "The stress will calm back down, once you're safe."

She raised her gaze from her plate, looked at him, and smiled. "I'd like to think so, but it won't happen anytime soon. Every time I close my eyes, even right now, all I can see is the guards," she said softly. "There's that sense, even when you're locked up in your room, that you are waiting for something to happen. And, of course, in our case, we were waiting for them to open the door, without notice, to either bring food in or to let us out, but letting us out would only take us back down to the lab again. There was no freedom. There was no sense of peace inside. Always this tension that just coiled up tighter and tighter and tighter."

"And so you can understand why Paul may have done what he'd done?"

"If he did that," she emphasized the last bit of it, "then yes."

"Do you think Marge would have?"

She raised her gaze again, looked at him, smiled, and said, "In a heartbeat. Marge needs to get out of here."

"We're taking her home." He nodded at the food. "Do you want some more?"

She shook her head, patted her tummy, and said, "I'm fine. I don't want to get woken up because I can't digest the food that I've had."

He stood and started packing up the food to put away in the fridge.

"How long are we staying here?"

"Not long," he said. "The faster we move and put some distance between us, the better."

"I'm actually surprised we're here, sitting in China still."

"Yes. But, if you think about it, they'll also expect us to make a run for it."

She nodded. "I would love to make a run for it."

"But now we have the Russians and the Chinese involved."

"I don't understand how the Chinese got involved, and now I really don't even understand how the Russians got into this."

"And we've sent out messages, letting them know that their Russian scientist didn't make it, hoping that will call off the Russians again, but there's no guarantee."

"I know," she said. "I just … To realize that you're in trouble with one group, only to find out you're in trouble with two, is a whole different story."

"The Russians, even if they had found you, may have completely ignored you," Diesel said. "You have to keep that in mind. They would have rescued their scientist and not likely done anything for you guys."

"They wouldn't even let us out?"

"They might have. No way to know. They might also want to keep this quiet, and they could have shot you."

At her shocked gasp, he nodded grimly. "Often in scenarios like this, it's a best-kept secret, but that means that everybody needs to be incapable of telling opposite tales."

Looking a little green, she stood and said, "I think, on that note, I'll go lie down."

"You do that," he said. "And, if you need anything, let us know."

She turned, looked at him, and said, "Thank you."

Surprised, he smiled and said, "You're very welcome."

"I mean it. I kept hoping that there would be a rescue. I kept hoping and telling the others that somebody would come, but they'd heard it all before. They'd had all their own hopes and wishes dashed for months and months on end," she said. "So I knew that they didn't believe me, even though

I was trying so hard to be positive, but it is hard to be positive in that situation."

"Absolutely it is," he said, "but it's all good now. Don't worry about that."

She smiled, nodded. And, on that note, she turned and headed to her bedroom.

As he returned to the empty table and brought his laptop back out again, Jerricho joined him.

"What do you think?" Jerricho asked Diesel.

"I don't like Marge's health at all," Diesel said.

Jerricho nodded. "I saw that. I don't know if she's even aware. She's not quite there yet mentally."

"Well, she's been through extreme trauma, stress. This kind of pressure can really play on you. Even if she is aware, she also knows there's nothing that she could have done about her health in those conditions."

"How do you want to get back home again?"

"Safely," he said. "There's no rush, other than a doctor to see about Marge, and we just have to stay low."

"No word that the Chinese have heard about Eva's rescue. Which confirms our theory that the gunfire we heard in the lab was the Russians taking out everyone in that place."

"Anything from the Russians?"

"Confirmation of the message about their dead scientist, but that was it."

"That's not helpful."

"No, but it is what it is," Jerricho said. "I've just brought up a series of exit options for us. We can go through mainland China. If we want to take a really long and slow route, we can cross over to Thailand, take an international flight or do some hopping across Asia, or we can go via water."

Instantly Diesel said, "Water."

"I agree with the water thing, but it'll take time."

"But we're also not in a rush, given a doctor on board, and then, if we could hook a ride on something that's got enough security, we wouldn't have to worry about being attacked."

Jerricho looked at him in surprise. "What are you thinking?"

"Well, I don't suppose a US sub or destroyer is around that we could hitch a ride on?"

He shook his head and laughed. "Let me ask." He went to the chat, opened it up, and immediately made a request for a pickup via naval vessel. There was no immediate response. He looked at Diesel and said, "I'm not sure that they liked the idea."

"I don't think *liking it* is an issue," he said. "I think it's a case of checking to see who and what's in the neighborhood and what their routes are."

"Even if we could get one back into Europe …" he said.

"We'll do the usual—dye everybody's hair, change their clothes. Get them some camouflage, so that the Chinese won't pick them out immediately. Help us gain a few hours. And see if we can get them somewhere safe."

At that, the chat spit out information, and the route that came up made Diesel laugh. "That's the same destroyer I came in on," he said. "And we'll rendezvous with a sub, and go the last several hundred miles that way."

"Perfect," Jerricho said. "Although it'll be very close confines for the women."

"But there should be a good medical center on the destroyer. Maybe we can get Marge looked at."

"Good point," he said. "But, if they find something critical, she'll need faster medical care than a slow-winding journey."

"Then we'll leave her with the destroyer, and they can take her on and off as they need to."

"That should make her happy."

"We also have to understand that the Russians and the Chinese may not stop looking for Eva or Marge or their next replacements, just because we've left," Diesel said.

"Meaning?"

"Meaning, I'd like to blow up the lab," he said bluntly.

Jerricho looked at him and then nodded. "I wanted to do it on our way out, but we had extra baggage with us."

"Which is why I was thinking this morning." He checked his watch and said, "As in, I would suggest six hours."

"Do we have enough C-4?"

"Only if we're smart with it," he said.

And, with that, they brought out the blueprints again on the building, where the labs existed. It took them an hour to work out a route and another hour to work out the logistics of how to maximize the ability to take down the entire building. As they sorted through their gear and stacked up and packed what they needed, Jerricho asked, "Did you consider other people could be in the building?"

Diesel nodded. "I did. If it's part of the lab, employees, that's one thing, or even guards," he said. "I just don't want there to be more scientists."

"What about clearing the building first?"

"We could. Smoke in the HVAC system?"

"That'll just knock them all out, still inside. We could do a prep bomb first, send out a warning, and, if anybody wants to run out, they can," he said.

He stopped, looked over at Jerricho, and said, "Wait, hang on. We should get some heatsink alerts from the satellites to let us know who and what's there."

"I don't know about through the satellite," he said, "but we should find out just what heat is inside the building now."

Diesel walked back to his laptop and started rapping out orders, looking for information on occupants within the building.

Shane came back with **Give us a minute.** A few moments later he texted, **The building's reading empty.**

He looked at Jerricho and said, "As far as I'm concerned, that means we need to go now, before they start refilling it."

"Taking the building down doesn't mean they won't just take over another building for their purposes," Jerricho reminded him.

"Maybe, but it also lets them know that people know what they're doing and won't stand for it."

"Symbolic?"

"If symbolic works, I'll take it," he said.

With that, they packed up and prepped to leave. As they checked and synched their watches, Diesel heard a voice behind them, turning to see Eva, standing in her bedroom doorway. "Hey," he said. "Couldn't sleep?"

She frowned as she looked at the gear they had on and their duffle bags near them. "You're leaving?"

"Yes, but not for long," he said. "We'll make sure the lab can't be used anymore."

Her eyes lit with understanding. She smiled and said, "Thank you for that. I wanted to destroy it but …" And then she stopped, shook her head. "It still won't stop the system."

"No, but it does send a message that they will be found out and stopped, if they do it again."

"I don't think they'll care," she murmured.

"Maybe not," he said. "Are you against us doing this?"

"No, of course not," she said. "I'm definitely for it."

"Good," he said. "Stay inside. We'll lock the doors, and, with any luck, we'll be back in less than an hour."

"And you're not expecting anybody to come?" She looked nervously at the front doorway and around the apartment.

He shook his head. "No. Throw the bolts, stay locked inside, go back to bed."

She took a long slow deep breath and said, "I guess that's the thing. Nobody knows we're here, do they?"

He shook his head. "No, you're free and clear here."

"Okay, good then." As she headed back to bed, she stopped, looked at him, and said, "You'll be safe, right?"

He looked at her and smiled. "We'll be fine," he said. "And so will you."

She beamed a smile, walked over, gave Diesel a great big hug, and said, "Thank you." She walked to Jerricho, gave him a hug, and said, "And, please, both of you come back. I can't imagine what we would do if you didn't." And she turned and walked back to the bedroom.

As they walked out and locked up behind them, Jerricho said, "I see she goes to you first."

"I was closer," he said in a noncommittal voice. No way he would let Jerricho know that he had thought the same thing.

"Ha!" he said, "This is good. This is really good."

"No, it's not," he said.

"Absolutely it is. I heard all about the pairings going on

with the Mavericks." He said, "I figure, by the time it's my turn, maybe there'll be a partner out there for me."

At that, Diesel turned and looked at him in surprise. "You want a partner?"

"Hell yeah," he said. "Been alone for a while. I had started a new relationship not long ago, but then I was called out on another mission and just realized how impossible it is. But all the Mavericks seem to be making it work."

"And I'm not exactly sure how that is either," he said, "because, when I was the second in command, I was always in the background. Now it's my mission, and I don't know what comes after this, with the Mavericks."

"That's okay," Jerricho said. "I think that's part of the joy. Just let it be."

"Maybe. At the same time, it's a little bit unnerving to not know what comes after this."

"Must you have your future locked down?"

The men quickly exited the safe house building, finding a new getaway vehicle awaiting them, courtesy of the Mavericks. They drove back to the warehouse district of Shanghai, parking several blocks away, and skulked through the shadows. When they arrived at the corner, the building in front of them, Diesel shook his head and said, "To your question, no, absolutely not. I actually prefer a little bit of surprise in life."

"So then be open to a little more surprises," Jerricho said.

And the two of them raced through the night.

CHAPTER 5

EVA WOKE SEVERAL hours later to an odd sound in the apartment. She bolted out of bed and hid behind the door. It took that long for her brain to remember that the men had gone out to demolish the building where they'd been held. She hadn't heard any explosions, but would she, this far from Shanghai? Probably. With enough dynamite, right? She trusted that these men could do the job.

After what she and Marge had been through—and Paul and everybody else—she was more than happy to see the lab go down. It wouldn't stop the system but … Then she heard another footstep in the hallway. Was it them? How could it be anybody else? She peered around the corner. As soon as she saw Diesel, she cried out in relief.

He looked at her, smiled, and said, "We're back, and it's just us."

She raced forward, shaking in relief. "I was so afraid," she said. "I woke up to a strange noise, and I didn't know what I heard."

"It's just us," he repeated. He reached out, wrapped an arm around her shoulders, tucked her up close, and said, "If you're tired you can go lie down. You've still got few hours yet until morning arrives."

"I know," she said. "I know. But, at the same time, I just don't really want to go through that kind of awakening again." She rubbed the sleep from her eyes and asked, "And was your mission successful?'

"Yes, the foundation's damaged, and it's on fire right now."

Even in the distance, she heard sirens, hopefully going to the lab but not too soon. "Good," she said. "At least they won't refill those basement rooms with more captives so easily."

"Nope," Jerricho said. "And we've almost got your escape route planned out too."

She looked at him, smiled, and said, "Now that would be great news. I can't wait until we get out of here."

"And it's happening today. We decided to move the schedule as fast forward as we could," he said. "It'll take a little bit of hopping around though."

"Right," she said, "but hopefully it won't be too bad."

"No."

She looked around and said, "Should I wake up Marge?"

"We'll need two hours, and we are planning on leaving, if we get everything okayed, before nine this morning."

"You don't want to leave in the dark?"

"No, in this case, we're better off to leave in broad daylight." He looked at her, winced, and said, "How do you feel about dyeing your hair?"

She looked at him blankly for a moment, her hand reaching up to her blond locks. "I guess that would make sense, wouldn't it?"

"Anything we can do to keep you out of the limelight would be good."

She smiled and nodded. "Did you get any box dyes?"

"They were just delivered," he said, "along with some sunglasses, skin toner, and a change of clothes."

"Perfect," she said. "I'm good with that. What about Marge? Her too?"

"Yeah," he said, "and it will take us a little bit to get your long hair done, so better we need to get started then if you want a nap afterwards we can make that happen."

"Perfect." She was surprised that the men seemed to be quite capable of doing the dyeing, as she thought she would have to do her own hair. They actually did it for her. By the time she was done, her hair dyed jet-black, Marge had woken up, and hers was almost done. Breakfast had also been delivered, and they had eaten. She looked over at the men. "You're not dyeing your hair?"

"Not yet," he said. "We'll change our hats, glasses, clothing."

"Right. Are we going as tourists?"

"Just being the four of us will already make us a little more visible," he said, "so we'll split up and do two and two."

"As long as all four of us get out of here safely, I don't mind," Eva said.

Marge looked over at Jerricho. "You think that's safe to split up?"

"It is," he assured her.

She smiled and said, "Fine."

As they packed up from breakfast, Eva looked around and said, "Do we have to clean this apartment?" she asked. "It's got our fingerprints and everything."

"A team will come in," he assured her.

She looked at him in surprise. "You have teams over here?"

He grinned. "We have teams all over the world."

"Fine," she said. "In that case, I'm happy to leave it

then."

And, with that, the women went and got changed. Eva almost smiled when she came back out in jeans and a black T-shirt and, with her black hair, her white skin shone almost too brightly.

Diesel immediately handed her the skin toner, and she understood.

"Right." And she quickly added a slight tan to her skin. It took the whiteness off and made her blend in a little bit more. And, with a big sun hat and sunglasses completing the look, she laughed as she stepped into flip-flop sandals. "Now this is very touristy," she murmured.

"It works," he said.

At that, the two men quickly loaded up on weapons that they could hide on their person, and she watched with interest as handguns went around ankles and into back shoulder holsters.

She said, "What about the rest of it?"

"The team will handle it."

"Right, the team," she said, "that nameless team I don't know anything about."

"And hopefully you never will. Because, if we have to bring in the team again," he said, "it means that there are more problems."

"I'm fine to leave them nameless," she said immediately.

He grinned at her, then looked at Jerricho and said, "I'll go out first."

"Rendezvous is in one hour and forty minutes," he reminded him.

"We'll be there. See you on board." And, with that, he held out a hand and said, "Come on, my dear."

"Oh, don't tell me," she said. "Are we husband and

wife?"

"We don't have any rings for that," he said, with a grin, "but we're partnered up anyway."

She chuckled, tucked her arm into his elbow, and, with more confidence than she actually felt, headed to the front door with him. They disappeared out into the early morning streets. She smiled, lifted her face, and said, "It's amazing just what freedom can do for your soul."

"We're not meant to be locked up," he said seriously. "Nothing about that is good for any of us."

OUTSIDE, DIESEL WALKED casually, his hand holding hers, tucked up against his body, talking to her in a calm voice, as they moved through the streets in the early hour. The traffic was just starting to pick up. He had no doubt that cameras were all around, but he wore a hat, and so did she, even though that would pinpoint them by looking a little odd. He was also counting on it blurring their features for at least a little bit. As they walked across the street, she asked, "How much farther?"

"We're taking a roundabout way," he said, "so it's a little bit yet."

"Well, that's good to know," she said with a laugh. "I was afraid this was the way that you always walk."

"Nope," he said with a gentle smile.

She beamed up at him. "Did I say thank you for the rescue?"

"Many times. If you're going to do it again, how about you thank me when we're out of here," he said drily.

"Yeah, good point," she said, her smile falling away.

He was sorry about that, but it was important that everybody stayed focused. They weren't on holiday right now, and they were still in grave danger.

"Did you guys figure out how we're getting out of here?" she asked, looking around.

"Absolutely, and it'll be a method that surprises you."

"I don't care how we get out," she said. "A plane would be great though. Fast and simple."

"There's nothing fast and simple about this. You're not in any rush to get back to the US, are you?"

"Well, yes," she said. "I want to get back to work, but, more than that, I'll go spend some time visiting my father."

"I like the sound of that," he said. "Just what does your dad do?"

"Now? Nothing," she said with a laugh. "He's retired, and it's a good thing too. He was getting burned out. Long ago, after Mother died, he just needed to have a break at the cabin, handed down to each generation in our family. And once he retired and ended up permanently at the cabin, our old famous fishing-hole cabin, I think he just never wanted to get back out into the real world."

"He lived in the real world long enough," he said, "and found out that it was shitty at times. You can't blame him for wanting to stay someplace that makes him happy."

She looked at him in surprise. "That's very true. He dedicated a lot of his life to research, medical research. I certainly don't begrudge him any of his decisions," she said. "It's just been a challenge."

"Of course, and you miss him."

"I do, and sometimes I bury myself in my own work too long and too hard," she said. "Going to Wisconsin to visit Dad would be a welcome break."

"And a much-needed stress relief," he said. "Do you like fishing?"

"You see? I *like* fishing," she said, "but my dad is addicted to fishing."

At that, he burst out laughing. "One of those guys up at five a.m. to go out and catch the early birds, by any chance?"

"Up at five a.m., out on the water by five-fifteen a.m. He'll take a thermos of coffee, sit there for a few hours, come home, might fuss around the house for a little bit, but then he'll go back out again, depending on what day, the weather, maybe for an hour, maybe for a few hours."

"I sure hope he likes to eat fish," Diesel said. He led her down the boardwalk toward the docks.

"He does like to eat fish, and he eats a fairly simple diet. He'll have trout and fried potatoes for breakfast, and he'll have cold trout on a slice of bread for lunch, and, depending on the day, he'll have grilled trout and maybe some barbecued veggies for dinner."

He looked down at her and said, "Are you ready for a full diet of fish?"

She wrinkled up her nose at him. "I like to fish as much as the next person. I just want to eat three meals a day of a more diverse menu."

"Lots of fishermen don't actually like to eat the stuff," he said. "It's all about the sport."

"That was my mother's doing. She said, if he would be bringing it home, he would be eating it, or she wouldn't have anything to do with it."

"Smart woman," he said.

"She didn't like to see waste, refused to let him take home anything that wasn't the right size because she said that the fish all needed an extra shot at life to get bigger. Yet the rules were just guidelines anyway, he would tell her, but she would continue her argument. In that case, then you make sure you toss back anything that wasn't at least the guideline level because he didn't need that fish. And, if he was the one having so much fun, he should do catch and release."

"And does he?"

"Lots of times, yes," she said, "but my mother trained him to do that."

"Good woman," he said. "I'm sorry for your loss."

CHAPTER 6

"**N**OTHING IS QUITE so difficult as losing your mother," Eva said, with a long sigh. "Especially the way I lost mine."

"I can only imagine."

She looked up at him. "Is yours still alive?"

"I never knew mine," he said with a shrug.

She stared at him in surprise.

"I was raised by my aunt and uncle," he said. "Story's a bit sketchy, but it sounds like my mother was a young partier, came home pregnant, had the baby, and walked. They figured it was more because she didn't want to come home and deal with the fallout of walking away."

"Were they good to you?"

At that, his face broke into a big smile. "They were the best," he said. "I can't imagine what my life would have ended up like without them. They were a very strong guiding force. And, of course, with my biological mother so wild and wooly, they were very much into teaching me responsibility."

"Particularly personal responsibility, I bet," she murmured.

He smiled. "As far as they were concerned, that was a huge priority in the world."

"And it is," she said, "as long as they were also caring

and loving."

"They were good to me," he said. "They never had any of their own children, so I filled a gap for them that they never had a chance to experience before."

"That would have made a difference," she said. "If they already had a family, then you'd have been the odd man out most likely."

"Didn't happen, which is something I'm grateful for," he said. "It would have been lovely to have had siblings though."

"Did you ever find your mom and talk to her?"

"No, she never showed up again."

"So you don't even know if she's alive or dead?"

"No, I don't actually," he said. "It's crossed my mind several times that maybe I should check up on her, but then I always figured that, if she'd wanted me in her life, she would have said something about it a long time ago."

"Or she felt so guilty now that she's an adult and figured out what she gave up."

"She did contact my aunt and uncle when I was about eight or nine, wanted an update—which really meant she wanted money."

"For you?"

"For me or to stay away from them. Something along that line. They were pretty blunt in their response, which was 'Hell no.' And, if she tried to extort more money from them, they'd bring in the cops."

"Well, at least they called a spade a spade," she murmured.

"After that nobody heard from her again."

"Sorry. That does make your relationship with your mom really about somebody who's only looking after herself."

"That's how I figured it too," he said. "I mean, maybe at one point in time, she'll reach out, but I can't say anything inside me pushes me to reach out to her."

"Well, if you ever change your mind," she said, "you can do so, as long as she's still alive."

"Maybe," he said. "She was also a drug addict and, for all I know, may have passed on from her addiction."

"I wonder what happens in cases like that? Would they contact anybody?"

"It depends if anybody even knows," he said. "So many people are out there in this world who don't have any human connection anymore, and the cops don't know who the next of kin are. Any number of unnamed, unclaimed bodies have been buried in unmarked graves."

THE TRIP WAS calm and peaceful. As Diesel and Eva headed down the boardwalk toward the docks, they heard a sudden loud *bang* to the side. She gave a slight yelp and jumped toward him. He wrapped her up in his arms and quickly pulled her close. She stood, trembling.

"I think it was nothing," he said.

"Well, it was definitely something," she gasped.

His hard gaze studied the area. "I think it's kids with firecrackers."

She stared up at him. "Why would anybody let kids have firecrackers?"

He smiled. "It's different over here."

She shook her head. "Kids can still get hurt, no matter where they are."

He nodded and pulled her gently along the boardwalk and said, "Come on. Let's go." Only he saw that her calm and peaceful mood was gone. "It'll be all right," he murmured.

She nodded but stayed mute.

"Tell me about your work," he said.

"No," she said, "I don't want to."

"Why is that?"

"Because it's something definitely ..." Her voice nervous, a tremor snaking through it, told him just how she had been putting up a brave front, yet still living in fear inside. She whispered, "How much farther?"

"Five minutes," he said, leading her past a large group of people talking animatedly. His gaze never stopped searching. His phone buzzed. He pulled it out to see a message from Jerricho. "They're there."

"Seriously? We're behind?" She picked up the pace, trying to drag him forward.

"Yes, but it's all right," he said soothingly. "We're still waiting for a boat to pick us up."

She looked at him in surprise, her feet automatically slowing to match his pace. "So getting there early won't help?"

"Not only will it not help but they also won't be there when we get there either."

She shook her head at him. "How come everything's so cryptic?"

"In case we're being overheard," he murmured.

At that, she immediately snapped her lips together and stared at him mutely, and then she stepped in closer and walked, not saying a word.

He appreciated that. Brains were behind that beautiful

face. And even though she'd been through a traumatic event, she was holding on to her common sense. He just smiled and said, "It will be okay."

She shook her head. "Not until I'm home."

"I get that," he murmured, as they headed down the boardwalk and away from more of the traffic into one of the farthest back alleys.

She stiffened. "Surely this isn't a good place to be?"

"It's where we need to be," he said.

And just as she thought that the alley was getting darker and darker, he pulled her into the back of a store, through the store and out to the front, which was now a completely different walkway. Ahead of her, she saw the docks. "Ah!" she whispered.

"Exactly." He squeezed her arm and said, "Come on. Let's go." And he led the way down one of the piers.

As they approached the water, she asked, "Does that mean that they're gone and that Marge's safe now?"

"Not yet, but she's getting there."

"How long until we join them?"

He nodded discretely to a Zodiac out in the ocean, going away from them. "They're on that."

She stared at it. "I wish we were too," she said softly.

"No need," he said. "We'll be on our own."

She looked up at him. "I don't understand how you can command all these resources."

"You'd be surprised," he said. "At least Uncle Sam's money is being put to good use."

She smiled bravely at that. He continued to walk her toward the water. His gaze searched the harbor, looking for their ride. As she stood stock-still beside him, she asked, "Is that the military behind us?"

"It is," he said in a low voice.

"Chinese military?" she asked, her nervousness getting to her.

He walked slowly, gripping her fingers gently in his hand, as they walked down the pier. "Doesn't mean they're looking for us," he said.

"Doesn't mean they aren't either," she snapped.

He loved the grit showing up every time her back went up. "You're right," he said, "but chances are, they don't even know anything about us."

"But what if they do?"

"Then we might have a bit of a skirmish," he said. "I'm looking for our ride right now."

She sucked in her breath and almost held it.

"Relax," he said.

"But they are coming up behind us."

He walked to the side of the pier, where there was a bench, and positioned himself where he could turn and defend her behind him. He also saw their ride approaching from the side.

What they needed was a few moments to get on it quietly and calmly, without suspicion. He studied the layout of the pier, noticing the military police were about one hundred yards away and closing in. There was no pause in their walk. There was no determined look on their face.

"I don't think they even know we're here," he said.

"I really don't want to take that chance," she said nervously.

He gripped her fingers and said, "I need you to stay calm. I need you to not let them know anything is different. We can't alert their attention to us."

She took a long slow deep breath. "I guess that's what

happens when you're kidnapped and taken captive," she said almost bitterly. "You become forever worried about what's … when it'll happen again."

"It won't happen on my watch," he said.

"You don't know that," she said. "You can't hold both of them off."

He looked down at her, his lips turned in a crooked smile, and said, "I wouldn't be so sure about that. But I don't want them to be aware that we are, in any way, anything other than tourists."

At that, her gaze was caught by something in the water.

He looked over and smiled. "Yes, watch the fish," he said and pointed a little farther out to another swarm, a school of fish that he couldn't name.

"Mother Nature's beautiful," she said, with a murmur.

"Not only is she beautiful but she's also very good at what she does."

"What, kill?" she asked, almost a snarl to her voice.

"There are always predators in this magical kingdom," he said. "The trick is to make sure you're not at the bottom of the totem pole."

"Maybe," she said, "but I was put at the bottom, so it's a little bit odd to even be thinking that I'm trying to get out of it."

"I get it," he said. "Hold strong."

She nodded slowly. As the men came closer and then walked past, she slowly let out her breath. "That," she said, "was not very comfortable."

"They'll have to turn around and come back as well," he said, turning her in his arms and pointing out more fish that were brilliant works of art. Up along the water, several junk boats were coming, some full of wares to peddle to the tourists and locals alike.

She smiled. "It must be an interesting life to live on a boat like that."

"I don't know about interesting," he said. "It'd be fun for a while. But I think you might get a little more feeling of being closed and hemmed in."

"Do you think so?"

"Well, in your room, you couldn't get out," he said, "but, when you're out in the water in one of those, you really have no place to go either."

She thought about it and nodded. "I guess you always think that you're in a big wide-open sea, under the blue sky, and you won't feel that same feeling. But, because you can't get off, maybe you do."

"It's exactly how it feels, yet, on the other hand, it is home for many, many thousands of people."

She nodded. One junk boat in particular pulled up in front of them and pointed at his wares. She smiled and shook her head.

As it was, Diesel smiled and gently pushed her down one of the ramps and said, "Let's take a closer look." And leading her down the wooden steps, they approached the area, where all the junks were lined up. He said, "Don't look around."

"Now I just want to," she snapped.

"Doesn't matter if you want to or not," he said. "They're watching us." They walked up to the first boat, and he studied the fruit. "Do you want a piece of fruit?"

"I don't think I could eat anything," she said.

He nodded and smiled and dickered for a piece and quickly picked it up and handed it to her.

She looked down at the pineapple and smiled. "Well, I do happen to like these."

"Good," he said. He kept walking, as if toward the other boats, as if wondering what the other boats might have for sale.

"I guess you can get anything here, can't you?"

"Literally anything," he said.

She sighed. "Have they left yet?"

"They've walked past, yes," he said.

"Great. Now what?"

He pointed at the junk boat ahead of them. "Now we're getting on this one." He stopped and turned to watch the two military police, but they were at the beginning of the dock and were talking to a group of men. He quickly ushered her inside the junk boat and had her sit under the overhang. She tucked inside, and he was beside her. The junk pushed away from the dock in a slow, gentle movement, just like all the rest, and very quickly they were milling around in the water, one of many junk boats.

She looked at him and said, "So Marge gets to go on a Zodiac, and we're on a junk."

"Yep," he said. "I wanted to make sure that nobody would have any reason to look for another Zodiac."

"I get that," she said, "but we'll never get anywhere at this speed."

He just smiled at her and said, "Oh ye of little faith."

She rolled her eyes at him.

He said, "Sit down, relax, and just enjoy."

CHAPTER 7

EVA COULDN'T BELIEVE how her world had flipped, and here she was now, sitting in a Chinese junk boat out in the harbor, casually floating along. She didn't know who the pilot was. All she knew was that Diesel was right beside her, completely unconcerned. It took time, but slowly she felt some of the tension easing off her shoulders.

When she finally took a deep breath, he smiled at her and said, "Feel better?"

She nodded. "I'd feel better yet again if we were farther away."

"Well, surprise, surprise," he said, "that wish is about to happen."

She looked up at him and looked around and said, "I can't see anything."

"But you didn't see the junk boat coming at you either, did you?"

She smiled. "No, that's true."

As it was, they pulled up to a powerboat, as if selling wares again. Instead she was escorted onto the powerboat, and he joined her. She watched as the junk boat then pulled away, and she was seated a little bit lower than normal height, had she sat on deck. Not quite down below but where nobody saw her. And the boat fired up and took off at a fast speed out toward the ocean. "Now where are we going?"

"The same place that Marge is," he said.

"I hope so," she said quietly. "I want to make sure she's okay."

"Well, we're working on it," he said.

She nodded. And it wasn't very long, and they saw a destroyer—a huge naval ship—in front of them. "Wow," she said. "Am I going on that?"

"You are," he said cheerfully.

She shook her head. "Almost nobody gets to go on these."

"No, they don't, not unless there's a purpose." He said, "In this case, you have a purpose, and we are cleared to go on board."

Getting on board wasn't as easy as it sounded, but she made it, and, by the time they were led through a series of small narrow hallways and stairs, they came to a door. With a hard rap, the door was opened. She was nudged gently inside, and Jerricho waited for them.

She smiled up at him. "Hey," she said, "I still don't quite understand how we got here, but we're here."

"And you should be feeling much more secure," he said. "You're on a US Navy destroyer. It won't be easy for anybody to take you off here."

She thought about it, nodded, and said, "You know what? That's one of the best pieces of news I've heard in a long time. Where's Marge?" she asked.

At that, his smile fell away.

"Please tell me that she's okay," she cried out.

"Well, it's not so much that she's okay or not okay," he said. "She certainly arrived here safe and sound. However, I don't know if you noticed, but she's got some health issues.

So she's in the medical center right now, getting checked over by the doctor."

Eva took a long slow deep breath. "I thought I saw a couple lumps, but, when I asked her about them, she wouldn't talk to me."

"No, and she's been pulling that same silent treatment and wouldn't discuss anything with me. In fact, I think she felt like I was a bit of a turncoat for taking her to the medical clinic."

"But it would make sense to have her checked over," Eva argued. "I mean, we have to think about how long she was a captive there."

"Exactly," Diesel said. "And, on that same note," he said, "we'll take you in and get you checked over."

She rolled her eyes. "I wasn't there all that long."

"Doesn't matter," he said. "We're also checking for subcutaneous tracking devices."

She looked at him in shock. "In that case, shouldn't you have checked us at the apartment?"

"We actually did," he said, "but they have better software here."

"Great," she said. "Because, if they'll track us here, isn't that seriously bad news?"

"You might want to think about exactly where you are right now," he said.

"True." She turned to follow Diesel back out again. As she walked, she asked, "Do I have to?"

"In the spirit of cooperation," he said, "absolutely. They can force you, but remember. You're a guest, and they have allowed us on board as part of your rescue."

"Right," she said, "and it is probably the right thing to get done."

"It absolutely is," he said. "You have no idea what you might have been fed or given or injected with, when you were out cold. We just don't know."

She shivered at the thought. "I really don't like the idea of a tracking device. I was just hoping to be as far away from that nightmare as possible."

"All it'll tell them, if you're here at this point, is that we have successfully rescued you," he murmured. "That might make them pissed, but they can't come up against a destroyer to get you back."

She nodded slowly. "No, they won't," she said. "Honestly I'm not all that big a deal in this whole research mess anyway. I've never quite understood *why me*."

"Did you do the research alone?"

"No, I had a research partner."

"And who is this other person?"

"Her name was Allie," she said, "but she died in a car accident a few days before I was kidnapped."

At that, Diesel turned to look at her. "A car accident?"

She nodded. "It was terrible."

"Did you actually see her body?"

"No," she said. "Why?"

"Just wondering if she actually died."

As they walked alongside and headed toward another set of stairs, he let her go up ahead. She quickly ran up the stairs, happy to feel her muscles moving as well as they were. She glanced back at him and said, "I know it doesn't seem like all that long since we had any food …"

"After your checkup," he promised.

She nodded and saw the medical center up ahead. As she walked inside, a woman stood and smiled at her, and Diesel quickly introduced them.

"Good," the woman said. "I'm Dr. Cavanaugh. Come on inside. We'll give you a quick check over."

At that, Eva followed the doctor into a small room, but the first thing out of her mouth was, "How is Marge?"

"We've done a bunch of lab work and are running some tests," she said. "We don't have confirmation of what's going on yet."

With that, Eva had to be happy. "I hope she's okay," she fretted.

The doctor had Diesel wait outside, while Eva took off her shirt and pants, where Dr. Cavanaugh did a full exam. "And how's your strength? How are you feeling?"

Eva answered all the questions as best she could. "I'm not bad," she said, "but Marge's pretty rough. She's been there a lot longer, and she's in shock after what they did to the other scientist."

"And how are you feeling?"

"Well, I'd like to get the guy who kidnapped us all, but, other than that, I just want to go home," she said quietly.

The doctor smiled and said, "We'll take your blood work and run some tests, just to make sure everything's okay. You can get dressed now." And the doc walked out.

Quickly donning her clothes again, Eva stepped out of the exam room to find Diesel still waiting there. She walked over immediately. He wrapped an arm around her, tucked her up close, and said, "You okay?"

She nodded slowly. "Just feels odd."

"Lots of oddness right now," he said. "Just push through until it feels more normal."

She smiled up at him.

The doctor came back into the waiting room and smiled and said, "You're good to go."

"Thank you," she said, "and please let me know when you hear anything about Marge."

"She's asleep right now," the doctor said. "I'll tell her that you're here, when she wakes up."

"Thank you." She looked at Diesel, looked at the doctor, and asked, "Do you know how to contact us?"

"I do," she said.

As Eva walked out, she said, "Nobody seems to be terribly forthcoming."

"It's the military. You're a guest. You're not one of them," he murmured.

She nodded. "Coffee?"

"I can get a coffee," he said. "I don't know how long the next stage will take."

"And what is that next stage?"

Following Diesel, she was led to what seemed like the far end of the ship and back again. But it took another solid twenty minutes plus to get to where they were going. And finally he walked into a room, where she was asked to be seated at one of several tables in front of her, with all kinds of electronic equipment. Diesel sat calmly at her side. She stiffened and looked over at him. "Is this the electronic tracking device stuff?"

"Among others, yes." He reached over, laced his fingers with hers, and said, "Stand strong."

She nodded, swallowed. "I'll be fine." Just then her name was called. She turned to look at somebody standing in a doorway and hopped to her feet. "Yes, that's me."

He nodded and smiled and said, "Come this way, please."

She looked back at Diesel and asked, "Are you coming?"

He looked at her gently and said, "Not this time."

DIESEL WATCHED AS Eva walked hesitantly forward. The bond between them was growing. He wanted it to be strong so that she would listen, in case he needed her to move very quickly. Yet, at the same time, he didn't want her to become too dependent on him. And that felt wrong too because she was a hell of a lot of independent woman. … Besides, he liked her almost a little bit too much. He'd been on a lot of rescue missions but rarely with this kind of connection. It was usually a group of them, and the mission was fast in, hard out. This was a very different thing. There was a connection between him and her that he had been denying this entire time. When the seat beside him was suddenly taken, he turned to find Jerricho here. He smiled and said, "Hey. Did they find anything on Marge?"

"On Marge, no. Although there's some suspicious things in her blood that maybe the Chinese lab might have been experimenting on her with."

"The doctor just said that she was getting a bunch of lab tests done."

"Exactly."

"But nothing electronic?"

Jerricho shook his head.

"Good," Diesel said. "In that case, Eva should be fine too."

"And, of course, that matters, doesn't it?" Jerricho said in a teasing voice.

He just smiled and nodded. "To a certain extent, yes," he said.

"Getting hooked?"

"Nope. Obviously she's an interesting person, and I'm

happy that we got her out safely."

"Yeah, that's part of it," Jerricho said, his grin wide.

"I'm not going anywhere else," he said.

"Good."

He nodded toward the doorway. "How long was Marge in for?"

Jerricho paused, frowned, and said, "I'm not exactly sure. I left her here and then came back and got her."

"*Hmm.* An hour?"

"No, not that long. Maybe twenty-five minutes."

"Good." And he settled in to wait. "Have you done a debrief yet?"

"I did. And you'll probably still have to go through one too."

"Of course. I was hoping that you could do it."

At that, he laughed. "And I may have. Still not exactly sure how this system works."

"No, and nobody knows. And we don't have to report to anybody, which is great."

"And yet we're visitors on this ship."

"Exactly," he said, "so courtesy demands a certain amount of information. Eva's looking for coffee and food as well."

"That's a good sign," Jerricho said. "If she's hungry, she'll be regaining her strength."

"Her temper's doing just fine too," he said.

Jerricho grinned. "She does seem to have one of those, doesn't she?"

"Absolutely. And that's good. It'll keep her in good stead."

"I'm also hearing a hint of admiration."

"There's nothing *not* to admire," he said calmly. "She's

handled herself very well."

"They both have. I was afraid, after seeing their colleague killed, that it would have a really negative impact on them."

"I think Marge more so than Eva," Diesel said, "but then Marge looks like she has been through an awful lot."

"She has," he said quietly. "I'm not so sure that she'll make it."

Diesel looked at Jerricho in surprise. "As in, you don't think she'll live?"

"I think she's got a terminal disease. I don't think, or I don't want to think, that the Chinese had anything to do with it. I just don't feel like she's here long for the earth."

"That would be very depressing for Eva. Not to mention for Marge herself, who hasn't had much chance to do anything yet with her newfound freedom, after spending the last however many months in captivity."

"I know," he said, "and unfortunately it doesn't look like, you know, given the size of those lumps … I doubt she has more than six months to live."

Diesel sighed and sank back into his chair. "Well, I hope you're wrong," he said. "Everybody deserves to have a better ending to their life than this."

"Yes, but at least we got them out, and she has whatever time she has. Be better than dying alone in that lab."

Diesel winced at that. "Intel pick up anything yet?"

"No, the city is silent as usual. The cover story on the fire says an electrical fire started in the basement."

"Well, that's not exactly true," Diesel said.

"Communist news is meant to always keep the public in the dark. It's how they keep voter confidence," Jerricho replied.

"Except there's no voting," he said, with a smirk.

"Very true. But they rule by controlling the flow of information as they want it. Remember?"

"I remember," he said.

Just then the door opened, and Eva stepped back out. She walked toward the two men with a bright smile. "I'm done," she announced. "So where's that coffee?"

Diesel smiled, hopped to his feet, and said, "Come on. Let's go get you a cup." He looked at Jerricho. "Are you coming?"

"Absolutely," Jerricho said. "We also have to figure out if we're done here or what our plans are afterward."

"We'll be here for a little bit," Diesel said, "but you're right. We have to figure out the next leg of this."

"Next leg of what?" Eva asked suspiciously, as they walked to the mess area.

"Well, you're still not back in the US yet," he said.

"Can't we go on this ship?"

"It's not going there," he said.

She frowned. "And I guess they won't turn it around and take us there just because I need to go in that direction, will they?" she asked softly.

"Not only that," Jerricho piped up and said, "they could need to offload us pretty quickly. It depends on some of the commands being forwarded here." He added, "There's a general air of excitement around the place, as if something's up."

"Is it related to us?" she asked in a hoarse whisper.

"No, but, when they get a change of orders, they'll move quickly on that order. We will have an option either to get off or to go to the next port and then get off."

"Fine," she said, shaking her head. "Apparently I don't get any of the finer details in this mess anyway, so you guys decide what's the best way to handle it."

Diesel smiled, looked down at her, and said, "Just remember. You're not in the lab. You're not locked up. You're safe here. So, even if it takes us a few more days, it's really not an issue."

She nodded and said, "True enough. So what am I supposed to do? Just sit back and enjoy?"

"Absolutely," he said, chuckling. "Sounds like a plan to me."

CHAPTER 8

THE FIRST DAY wasn't an issue at all because Eva slept off and on for the next twenty-four hours. By the time she woke up on day two and headed for breakfast, Diesel at her side, she noted she was still being escorted. "So are you protecting me or the rest of the crew?"

He burst out laughing. "Basically nobody is allowed here without being escorted. You can't be allowed to wander at will."

"Ah," she said, "and I noticed that nobody's really saying anything to me."

"But they're not unfriendly, are they?"

"No, that's true," she said. "Just … it feels weird."

"Think of yourself as an invited guest."

"Well, that is how it feels," she admitted. "I guess I was hoping for a less formal atmosphere."

"The military does formal very well," he said.

She burst out grinning. "Do we have any news on Marge?"

"Nope, but, after breakfast, if you want, we can stop in and see how she's doing."

"I'd like that," she said. "I did stop in yesterday with Jerricho for five minutes, and she was happy to see me, but I think she was also happy to see me leave."

"She's tired, exhausted. Her system's on overload," he

reminded her.

"I know," she said. "I just want to make sure that she'll be okay."

"She'll be as okay as the US Navy doctor can assure us that she'll be okay."

"She might have to go on a different flight home again anyway, I suppose. She was taken from Australia. So it depends where we end up."

"You mean, where she wants to go, yes," he corrected.

"Exactly that. We're not limited to going back to the US." As they walked into the cafeteria, she smiled and said, "And, of course, we're just at the end of the mealtime, aren't we?"

"Again it's easier on everybody."

She nodded, quickly walked up to the food, and served herself, with a little help from the chef on the other side. With a bright smile, she walked over, picked up a coffee, and sat down at a table away from everyone.

Diesel and Jerricho joined her immediately.

"So tell me why again Marge'll go one way, and we'll go another?"

"It isn't for sure yet," Diesel said. He hesitated.

Jerricho looked at him and said, "She might as well know."

"Know what?"

"The doctors suspect that she's got a terminal illness and that she doesn't have very long to live. There was talk about sending her, with her permission, to a center in Switzerland, where she might get some treatment," Diesel said.

"Wow," she said, sitting back in shock. "When did you find that out?"

"This morning," Diesel said.

She nodded and stared down at her food. "That seems so unfair," she cried out softly.

"Remember? Life isn't fair."

"I know," she said, "but sometimes it's really a bitch."

"It is. Eat up, and we'll go see her."

"Is this likely to be the last time I do see her?"

The two men looked at her and said, "Why don't you just not focus on that?"

She didn't even know what to say. She managed to get some food down but only half of what she had taken. She stared at it and said, "I can't get any more down. I'm too upset over Marge."

"I understand," he said. "Let's go talk to her, and see how you feel afterward."

And, with that, they got up and left the table.

As she walked out, she turned to look up at him. "So am I going to Switzerland too?"

"Do you want to go to Switzerland?" Diesel asked.

"No," she said, "I want to go home."

"Then we're going home."

She shook her head. "And when is that?"

"I'll let you know," Diesel said. "After you visit with Marge, I've got a meeting with the captain."

And, with that, Jerricho turned and walked away.

She looked at Diesel and asked, "Now what?"

"I'm taking you to Marge," he said gently.

"Okay," she said, "let's go."

DIESEL ESCORTED EVA through the ship back to the medical clinic center. As they walked in, the nurse looked up, frowned, and said, "I hope you're not here for Marge."

"Actually I am." Eva stepped forward, looking at the nurse in surprise. "Why? Is that a problem?"

"She was just flown out about forty-five minutes ago," she said, checking her watch.

"Oh no," Eva said, "I wanted to say goodbye."

"She took a turn for the worst," she said.

"Worse how?" Diesel asked.

"She's got stage four cancer. She seemed to think that she would never get away from her captives, so she hadn't worried too much about what the end result would be. But, once we managed to take a good look at her, she said that she'd known for quite a while."

"Oh no," Eva said. "I was really hoping for good news. And I was hoping to see her down the road in the future."

"I suspect that won't happen. She did want to make it back to Australia and die there. But the best medical help for her is in Switzerland. I don't know that she'll make the journey all that well. Only through her insistence and the officers in charge, who made some connections happen, is she even on her way. Otherwise I don't think she'd have survived very many more days."

When a faint cry came from Eva, Diesel immediately reached out for her. He tucked her up close and said, "I'm so sorry." He gently stroked her shoulder, and she stared up at him wordless. "I know you didn't know anything about it, and now it's such a shock."

"Why didn't she tell me?" she asked.

"Maybe she didn't want to face it herself."

Eva thought about that for a moment and then looked at him and nodded. "That's quite possible," she said, her voice careful and quiet. "She was never one to talk about herself."

"Exactly. For all you know, it's something that she's had for a long time, and, once she was kidnapped, she knew that, if she didn't get rescued right away, there wouldn't be any hope for a cure. Now that she was rescued, she probably already assumed it was too late."

Eva looked over at the nurse. "Do you have any contact information so I can contact Marge in Switzerland?"

"I'll ask for permission to share that with you," the nurse said. "Of course I can't do it without permission."

Diesel saw the distress in Eva's facial features. "Come on. Let's go back to your room." He turned around, met up with Jerricho, and nodded her in the right direction and, thanking the nurse, the three of them walked back to their rooms. When they got in, she sat down on the bottom bunk and stared up at him.

"It'll be okay," he murmured.

"Nothing'll be okay," she said. "Just think about that. I mean, she didn't even have a chance to enjoy her freedom."

"Nope, she didn't, and she wouldn't want you to be sitting here moaning about her either," he said.

She gave a bitter laugh at that. "Marge was very hard to get to know at all," she said, "but I know, in this last week or so, she just seemed to give up. I think she was getting sicker and sicker. I noticed the lump myself, when we were with her in the apartment. When she saw the look on my face, she changed her shirt, put on one of those heavier hoodie tops. She had lumps in several spots where there shouldn't have been any. Maybe I guess it's just the suddenness of it. I mean, I hope that there's still some treatment for her, and, if not, then I hope her passing is fast and painless," she said. She leaned her head against the back wall, her body now almost flat out on the bed. "When do we leave?"

"At ten."

She looked at him in surprise. "You already have something arranged?"

"Yes," he said, "I do."

"Great, and how long will we be at this next stop?"

"I can't really say much about that," he said. "It depends. I know this ship is getting underway and heading off on orders, so we can't stay here anyway."

"Right, and you're trying to keep me undercover as long as possible."

"Exactly," he said, with a smile. He looked at her with concern. "I know that Marge's leaving has hit you hard," he murmured, "but we need you to stay positive."

"I am positive," she said. "I would also be fully prepared to fly a commercial airline. Can you see if we can get on one? Once we're on and in the air, then we're pretty well home free."

"That might work," he said, "but, according to our intel, the Chinese government has locked down security even tighter."

"Do you think they're looking for us, or they're looking for the Russians?"

"If they know that you're missing," he said, "the Chinese will be looking for both us and the Russians. For sure, for the Russians."

"How are the Russians likely to get out of China?"

"A lot of different avenues," he said, "but, like you said, the fastest is by air. I don't know if they would try that right now, when there's so much security on the go."

"Fine," she said. "I'll just nap here for a while. You tell me whenever it's time to go, and I'll go."

He worried about the tone of her voice. He looked over

at Jerricho, who nodded toward the door. "Fine," he said, as he crouched and gently patted her knee. "If you want to talk, let me know."

She gave a startled laugh. "I don't even know what I'm supposed to do anymore," she said. "Everything's just flipped."

"Well, what we'll do," he said, "is get you to your father."

"And, for that," she murmured, "I would be forever grateful."

As the guys walked out the door, a seaman approached them.

"The captain wants to speak with you," he said in a low voice.

Diesel nodded, closed the door firmly behind him, and followed the seaman to the captain.

As they entered the small room, the captain motioned at them to sit down. "You're involved with the two women who were rescued, I presume?"

"Yes, sir."

"We had a helicopter remove the one woman just over one hour ago. She was being taken to the mainland and transferred to a medevac, where she would take a commercial air flight out. During the transfer, the medevac was shot down and crashed. All are presumed dead."

The words were so shocking that it took a moment for it to sink in. "Pilots? Doctors?"

"Yes, two of each."

"Crap, and there's no hope of any survivors?"

"No."

"And do you have any idea what happened?"

"The official version," he said, looking down at his pa-pers, "will be a freak accident."

"Unofficial?"

"A rocket launched somewhere close by," he said. "We're still working on satellite imagery to see if we can find out more."

"Damn." He looked over at Jerricho. "We're not going back onto the mainland then."

"No, but you do need to find alternate arrangements. We can carry you for another one hundred nautical miles, as we head toward the mainland, but you need to come up with another pathway to get your other passenger moved."

"We can do that," he said, thinking hard and fast. "The farther away from China obviously, the better."

"It was against our better judgment but, given her dire medical condition, we hoped that Marge would make it."

"I'm glad her death was quick, but obviously this is a terrible loss." Diesel stood and said, "If you'll excuse us, we'll go make travel arrangements. Are you rendezvousing with anybody we can hook up with?"

"Potentially, if you give me a travel plan."

"Will do."

They turned and walked out. Back in their room, Diesel sat down with a laptop and typed in the news to Shane.

A series of question marks came up. **I don't know if it's related or not.**

Of course it is.

I know. I'm trying to work on the whole denial bit. We need to get you out of there.

Obviously they know where Marge came from, so yes. I can't be seen. Eva can't be seen.

Suggestions?

Not yet.

Submarine? We can transfer you to another ship.

Still not one of the better answers.

One ship and you just hop along the way.

Or? He looked over at Jerricho. "We have to get off of here. If we go anywhere, we'll be dealing with an assumption that we came from the same ship as Marge. Anything close to us will be suspect."

"South Korea," he said instantly.

Diesel contemplated that. "Maybe as a jumping-off point. Otherwise Thailand? International airports, tons of tourists, travelers, less of a connection to China."

"Either is possible," he said. "Hong Kong's a mess right now, and we want to stay away from there. Vietnam?"

"Possibly." Diesel thought about it for a moment, and then he sent a message to Shane. **Either Vietnam, Thailand, or South Korea.**

Thailand.

That's what I was thinking, but we do still have to get there.

I know, he wrote. **If we can get you onto the Vietnam coast, then you can go through Thailand.**

Actually forget that Diesel typed. **Let's just do the Philippines.**

You don't think President Duterte will care?

He might care, but he won't do anything about it. We should get in and mingle.

You don't look the part.

I don't plan on staying. The Manila airport doesn't have very much security, so it's a good option too.

Fine, we'll arrange that.

Least amount of ships would be best.

It'll take what it takes. Be ready to leave immediately. I'll be back in touch with details.

With that, Diesel signed off. He looked over at Jerricho.

"How well do you know Manila?"

"Fairly well," he said. "You can buy anything you want, so that's a plus."

"Or a negative, depending on if anybody else is around, looking for us."

"Every airport in China will be watched, as are trains, yachts, ferries. All would be under heavy surveillance, and I would suspect that they'll have some intelligence going out to all their allies as well."

"It would make sense." So Diesel sat and wondered if the Philippines was even the right answer. "We have to make a choice. We can't get all the way home from here. Do you want to try commercial?"

"I'm not sure," Jerricho said. "I'd rather do a military base."

"We can do that too," Diesel said, and, with that plan set, they set down to work on the details.

"It'll be even more important to make sure we're not seen," Jerricho warned.

They thought about it for a long moment. "We still have to take a chance."

"Or we hook a ride on a submarine, take a slow boat out," he said.

Diesel smiled at that. "She might go for it, but I think she's already biting at the bit to get home."

"Not that she has a choice," Jerricho murmured.

"We could pick up some followers, if we end up cutting through the Philippines," he murmured.

"We could anywhere."

He shook his head. "Let's just do it."

With that agreed, he got up and walked back down to Eva's room. He knocked on the door, and, when a sleepy voice was heard on the other side, he winced.

She opened the door, stared up at him, rubbing the sleep from her eyes.

"I'm sorry," he said. "I didn't mean to wake you."

"I probably needed to anyway," she said, smothering a yawn. She pulled the door open wider and motioned for him to come in.

"Are you okay?"

"No, I'm not okay," she said crossly. "I won't be okay for a long time. It's hard to have seen Paul killed but now to know about Marge's cancer death sentence?"

He nodded and said, "And now I've got more bad news."

"What could possibly be more bad news?" she asked with a gasp.

He winced and said, "Come on. Sit down."

As she sat back down again, she looked at him. "What could possibly be wrong?"

"I hate to say it," he said, "but it's more bad news about Marge."

CHAPTER 9

EVA WATCHED AS Diesel opened his mouth and then closed it again. "Spit it out," she murmured.

"The plane carrying her, two doctors, and two pilots has crashed."

She stared at him, as she felt all her insides pulling in, tightening up, and shaking. "Marge was on board?"

"Yes, all five lost their lives this morning," he said quietly.

She looked at him and then looked down at her trembling hands.

He grasped her hands and tugged her a little bit forward.

She immediately got up and, following his movement, sat down in his lap, where she could bury her face against his neck and chest. She didn't even realize she was weeping for the longest time, but her sobs rocked her body up and down, as he slowly massaged and stroked her back.

"I'm sorry," he said. "I'm so sorry."

When she finally regained her voice, she sat up slightly, wiped her eyes, and said, "I mean, if it makes her ending easier, then fine," she said. "But I know she really wanted to go home to Australia. I don't know if she had family or something there that she was trying to get back to one more time. That's just so sad."

He nodded. "And we agree on that."

She looked at him for a long moment, then she said, "Please tell me this has nothing to do with what was going on in our lives first." He looked at her steadily, and her heart sank. "You're not telling me anything to the contrary, are you?" she whispered.

"I can't," he said. "Officially it'll be a freak accident, but, according to the captain, it was quite possibly a rocket launcher."

"Oh my," she said, her hand slowly going to her mouth, as she stared at him, wide-eyed. "What chance is there that I'll never get out of here alive?"

"I'm not sure," he said, "because we don't know how widespread this is. The bottom line is, we have a plan, and we'll head toward the Philippines, lose ourselves in Manila, and catch a flight out."

"We're hardly the right coloring."

"But we're not that far off," he said.

Then she nodded. "I didn't even notice," she said, reaching out for his now jet-black locks.

"All it does is give us a chance," he said. "We need every chance we can get."

"I'll take anything right now."

He said, "We might have another option, but it will take a long time. And I'm not exactly sure what we'll do."

"Meaning?"

"We could take a submarine back toward US waters."

"Oh, wow," she said, staring at him. "But that'll be weeks, won't it?"

"Exactly."

"Yes, okay. Let's try Manila," she said. "You'll look after me, right?"

"I certainly will," he said. "And, if Manila doesn't look

good, we'll find another way home."

"Fine," she said, staring at him, dry-eyed. "When do we leave?"

"Now," he said gently.

She looked at him in shock. "As in *now* now?"

"As in *now* now," he replied.

She nodded, glanced around, and said, "Well, I don't have anything to bring with me, so it's not like packing's a problem." She took a long sharp, deep breath, and said, "Sorry, Marge. That's not the end I would have wanted for any of us."

But Eva knew it was all too possible that her future was uncertain too. She didn't want to put any more pressure on the men because she knew that they were doing the best they could. But she really didn't want to end up in Marge's position. "I really hope we make it," she said, "and it makes me angry that I'm having to ask for somebody's help to stay safe. This nightmare shouldn't have happened in the first place."

"Another one of the reasons we're changing course."

"Fine," she said. "I'll use the washroom, and then we can leave."

She quickly used the facilities, and then, as he opened the door, she saw Jerricho, waiting for them on the other side. He led her out to the surface of the destroyer, where she was immediately buffeted by strong winds. She looked around for Diesel, who immediately grabbed her arm and tucked her up close. Shielded her with his body, he led them to a helicopter. She was assisted inside, and Diesel sat down beside her, quickly buckling her in. She snuggled up close, loving the security of having him here, knowing she shouldn't depend on that.

With the high winds, she wasn't even sure that they should fly. She wanted to ask them if it was safe, but then suddenly they were up in the air. She didn't understand that, but, as soon as they were skyborne, she realized that a lot of the wind she had felt on deck came from the rotors themselves.

As soon as they were up in the air, she settled down slightly, so she could look at the view. "Do you think any rocket launchers face us right now?"

He shook his head. "No."

"I hope not," she said. As it was, they ended up on a huge yacht several miles away. She looked at him. "This isn't military."

"No, it's just a stopping point."

The yacht quickly approached another craft, where they were put into a speedboat. At that, he lifted a hand in a goodbye wave, and then the three of them took off. Jerricho remained quiet but alert.

She twisted to look back at what could have been a multimillion-dollar superyacht. "Do you know them?"

"We might have touched bases once in a while," Diesel said, with a smile.

"You guys have friends in strange places."

"Strange friends in high places, all over the place," he corrected. "It's a good way to run a business."

"Maybe," she said, "just a little confusing."

"Only for those of you trying to make sense of it," he said. "Don't worry about it. Just look after yourself."

"I'm trying to," she said, with a little more spirit. "I'm determined to live. Paul and Marge didn't get a chance, but I refuse to become the third victim."

"Good," Diesel said. "I want you to hang on to that

thought, even when things get tough."

And she realized that, as far as he's concerned, things would get a lot tougher, and she wasn't sure she was prepared for it in any way. The speedboat bounced over the waves, even as the clouds moved in above them, and she felt a chill settling in.

Diesel noticed and sat close to her, wrapping an arm around her and pulling her up tight against his heavily muscled frame. "I'll make a windbreak for you, if you sit on this side."

She quickly changed positions and then noted he sat sideways, and he tucked her up between his legs and then wrapped his arms and legs around her—like being wrapped up in a heating blanket. Almost immediately her shivers settled down. "How come your body heat is so extreme?" she murmured. He laughed, his voice warm and deep against her ear. She leaned into it ever-so-slightly, a smile tickling at her lips, as she heard that voice.

"I don't know," he said. "I've always been the warm-body type."

"And I'm always the *socks in bed* type."

He burst out laughing. "Not my style," he said. "I have great circulation."

"Is that what the problem is?" she complained gently.

"I think so," he said, with that endearing smile of his.

She nestled in closer, greatly appreciating not only the strength but the heat and the emotional support and the surreal sense of just knowing she wasn't alone and that these guys were handling it, that they had it under control. And even though she didn't know what the heck was going on or how to stop this craziness in her world, they did. And that was good enough for her. She was willing to trust them right now, and, as long as they were willing to keep looking after her, she'd take all the help she could get.

As she watched the ship go through wave after wave, she asked, "Should we even be out here?"

"Yes," he said. "A ton of people won't be out here, but a lot who are will be racing to avoid the weather. A storm is coming up in the ocean."

At that, she twisted to look behind him. She saw the dark clouds gathering. Even as she watched that and studied the open water around her, she saw the white plume of other boats racing for shore. "Good timing," she said. "It really does look like we're just one of many."

"Exactly."

She settled in for the ride. But it did get colder and colder. She sat, numb, waiting for this to end. Finally they pulled up to one of the harbors and coasted along the shoreline, until they got to a spot that they had previously picked out. As they pulled up here, they were let off, and the pilot immediately raised a hand, turned around, and headed back out.

"Should he be going back right now? Is it safe?"

"He knows what he's doing," Diesel said. "I think he'll dock at another place on shore and then head back out, when the storm's over."

Feeling better about that, she nodded. "Well, that's good," she said. "I don't want him to get hurt because he had to bring us here."

"Don't worry about it," Diesel said. "They know what they're doing."

Since those were the same words he'd used a few minutes ago, she just nodded. Next, she found herself shuffled down the pier toward land, where they climbed up a winding path, past a series of huts, up to a road. A vehicle sat waiting for them. She stared at the vehicle, looked at them, and said, "Seriously?"

"Seriously."

Jerricho hopped into the driver's side, as she slid into the back seat, along with Diesel. She looked at him. "What's next?"

"Hoping to hit an airport tonight," he said. "We're checking availability."

"You didn't do that before?"

"We did, but no seats available. We need three."

"Right. We don't have to be together though."

He explained. "But we do need to have three on the same flight."

She nodded. "It's all about safety, isn't it?

"Absolutely," he said. "Remember. We got this. It's okay. If three aren't available today, we'll wait until tomorrow."

"So, in other words, you're expecting cancellations?"

"That's what we're hoping for, yes. There could be all kinds of reasons for not getting a flight," he said. "We just want to make sure that we have everything locked down."

She settled in beside him, happy to have him handle the details.

As it was, they pulled up to a small motel. She looked at it and said, "Hardly your terrorist-type hotel."

"We don't want one of those," he said. They parked around back, and she was escorted inside and straight to a room.

"So all you ever do is put out a request on your phone and get instructions back about where to go?"

"Sometimes it's a little more complicated."

"Like?"

"Like, when we have no communication at all," he said.

She winced at that. "I don't think I'd like that."

"It's happened several times to many of us already," he said. "So we take the communication when we can get it because it makes life easier. But we're fully prepared to go underground, if we need to."

She didn't want to ask what that meant because it sounded horrible. As it was, they were doing what they could do, and she would be okay with that. She walked into the room and counted just two beds. She took the one farthest from the door and threw herself down full length on it.

"Do you want to sleep, or do you want to eat?"

"I want to fly home," she said, "but, if that's not an option tonight, food would be good."

"Food's on its way," Jerricho said. He looked over at the two of them. "I'll step outside and check out the lay of the land." And, with that, he disappeared.

"What does that mean?" she asked, sitting up and brushing the hair off her face. She still wasn't used to her newly dyed dark locks, when she caught sight of them out of the corner of her eye. Not that she cared. It just was an unusual sight.

"He'll check to see if we're safe," he said, without pulling any punches.

She winced. "Meaning, we could have been followed?"

"I doubt it, but it's possible, or somebody has been alerted that we've left the country and are looking at all options."

"Still not a good answer," she murmured. She reached up and rubbed her face, then looked down at her clothes and sighed. "Any chance of a change of clothes?"

"For morning, yes," he said, studying her. "Wouldn't be

a bad idea for the flight anyway."

"Well, jeans and a black T-shirt are pretty universal," she said, with a laugh.

"But that's also what they're likely looking for."

"Right, so something completely opposite." She shrugged. "I'm sure you've got an answer for that too."

She walked into the bathroom, desperate for a shower and a refreshing mind shift. So she shed her clothes, hopped in the shower, and closed her eyes, as she stood under the hot relaxing water. If nothing else right now, at this moment in time, she was safe. She was okay and, although everybody else in her world apparently was messed up, she would be just fine. And, if she told herself that often enough, she might believe it.

DIESEL SAT AND waited while she had her shower. In the meantime, he checked in on the Mavericks chat window and asked for information and an update on Marge's death. The information started to flow, so he sat back and read. No doubt that it had been murder, but the details were still sketchy. They also couldn't confirm that it was connected to Marge and, therefore, possibly connected to Eva. Or was it connected to any of the other four people on the helicopter or just somebody who was disgruntled and chose a target?

In Diesel's mind, he figured it was most likely connected to Marge, but that was also just thinking and looking for a boogeyman everywhere. He asked for an update on the Russians.

No update. They haven't been seen.

He stared out the window and then muttered to himself,

"Could mean they're underground. Could mean they've been taken out. Could mean they've booked it and are safely home."

There was really no way to know. Outside of keeping track of his own mission, he couldn't do a whole lot. He had the photos of the two guards he had killed in the lab, both were Chinese though and could be tough to track. The Russian team that had been there would likely be easier. Shane had facial recognition on some of the Russians. On a whim, Diesel texted, **Can you run the Russians through the facial-recognition system in Manila?**

Sure, but not a whole lot of tech here.

I've got us booked on the last flight out tonight. We'll head to Australia, and then we'll take a flight back over the ocean.

Good enough, send the details.

With that done, he closed the laptop, got up, and stretched. He was hot, tired, and could use a good 10K run or, even better, a good hard swim. But those were not available, so this is what he had. He dropped to the floor and did several push-ups and then held a plank for a few minutes before doing several long yoga stretches. By the time he was on his last one, the bathroom door opened, and Eva stepped out, wrapped up in two towels.

He smiled. "Now," he said, "you look completely refreshed."

"Just don't look in my eyes," she murmured.

He nodded. "The soul takes longer."

"It does, indeed. But that's okay," she said with a smile. She motioned at him. "You're not the kind of person I ever thought would do yoga."

"Don't make judgments," he said with a grin.

"Not so much judgments," she said, "it just never occurred to me."

"It's really good for easing up the kinks in your system."

"Well, I've got plenty of that," she murmured.

He nodded. "And any time I can't get in a run or a swim," he said, "yoga offers at least something to help stretch and relieve some of the tension."

"Well, tension I definitely understand." She sagged onto the bed beside him, while he did several downward dog movements. "I used to do Sun Salutations every morning," she said. "I don't know why I stopped but after being in captivity I started again to save my sanity."

"Like everything, it's easy to forget, and you turn around, and weeks have gone by since you did your last session."

"I get busy at work," she said quietly, "and then I just blank out. Like you said, weeks have slipped by, and I didn't notice."

"Of course," he nodded. "I'm the same way. But right now I have a moment, so I'll take it."

"Since Jerricho's outside, checking things out around us," she said, "will he pick up food?"

"He will," he said.

"Any update?"

"No," he said, "not really."

She rolled her eyes at him and headed back into the bathroom. She held up her clothes and said, "I really don't want to put on these old clothes."

"Sorry," he said. Then he stopped. "I have a clean T-shirt, if that would make you feel better."

Her head popped around the corner. "Would you mind?"

He shook his head. "Nope, we have new clothes coming." He got up, walked to his bag, pulled out a simple white T-shirt, and handed it to her.

She smiled and said, "This is a huge gift." She stepped back into the bathroom. And, when she came out again, she was decently covered, with his T-shirt swimming down past her hips.

He grinned. "You look like my best friend's kid sister."

She looked up at him in surprise. "Funny. I didn't even think about you having a girl as a friend when you were younger."

"I don't anymore," he said, with a gentle smile, "but we were close while we had each other."

He didn't elaborate, and she didn't ask, but she looked at him questioningly a couple times.

He knew what that was like too. Because, when you got to know each other, you didn't really think about all the family ups and downs that came with other people's stories, but it was what it was. He'd loved her dearly. He hadn't been there when she'd been killed in a car accident, and that had broken his heart, but it was good ten years ago now. So, although he kept her close to his heart, it didn't tear him apart anymore. When he saw Eva still looking at him, he smiled and said, "I'm fine honestly. She was killed in a car accident over a decade ago."

She nodded slowly. "Still it's hard, isn't it?"

"As you know," he said, "it's hard to lose anybody you care about."

"Yeah, that's why I want to go see my father," she said. "The homesickness is really strong right now."

"To be expected, when you were locked up for however long."

"Right, and just knowing that I'm heading there and that I'm almost there, it's so damn tantalizing."

"We'll get you there," he said.

She nodded. "You know what? I believe you now."

He burst out laughing. "Well, thanks for the trust," he said.

"Yeah, I should have trusted you earlier too," she said, "but, for whatever reason, just with everything happening, it was really hard."

"I would expect it to be," he said. "Nothing like this is ever easy, and just so much is going on around you that you don't get a chance to adjust."

"No adjustment at all. We're just from one place to the next and then Paul and Marge. It was just really hard," she said sadly.

He looked at her. "And how are you handling it now?"

"I still think it's hard, but I'm dealing."

He nodded and said, "Good." He straightened out, shook his body, looked at her, and asked, "Would you mind if I stepped in and had a shower?"

She shook her head. "Go for it," she said. "Who knows when we get another one?"

"Exactly." He walked to his bag, grabbed a change of clothes.

She watched, as he walked by, and said, "I'm so jealous."

"You'll get new clothes tomorrow," he promised.

She shrugged. "I have a new shirt now," she said. "I'm almost wealthy."

Still chuckling at that, he walked into the bathroom and closed the door.

CHAPTER 10

E VA DIDN'T KNOW what to make of him. There was something so very personal about him, but, at the same time, he was a little more aloof and kept himself just that little bit disconnected from everything around him. But then she should recognize that because it's exactly the same damn thing she did.

Then the door opened again, and he stepped out, just wearing his jeans, and he handed over her earrings.

"Oh, my goodness," she said, jumping up to take them. "I always forget. I take them out, and then I completely forget about them on the counter."

"Well, here they are," he said, and he stepped back in.

But it wasn't fast enough for her to actually tear her gaze away from the incredibly muscled chest that he'd presented. He could have been a model for any of those romance covers that were everywhere. Or maybe one of those firefighter calendars. He was built. But then, given the job he did, she guessed fitness was of prime importance. She put her earrings on and walked to the window, where she could stare out.

She'd always wanted to do more traveling but hadn't expected to do it in this cloak-and-dagger method. As she stood here, waiting for him to finish in the shower, she wished she had her own personal laptop or phone, where she could check emails too. Just even to surf the web and to check out the news that she'd been disconnected from for a long time. She looked at his laptop, wondering if she could use it, but, since she hadn't asked, she didn't dare.

Just then she heard a sound outside in the hallway. She got up and walked closer to the door, wondering if it was Jerricho but didn't take a chance by opening the door. She stepped up to the door, wondering if she should let Diesel know. She heard another weird scraping sound, as if somebody were sliding along the hallway.

When the bathroom door opened beside her suddenly, she almost let out a squeak. Eyes wide, her hand over her mouth, she pointed at the door. Diesel, still wearing just jeans, with the towel around his neck, nodded and stepped forward. He used the towel to dry off the shaving cream off his chin, but he appeared to be completely unconcerned.

He listened at the door, and she heard the same scraping sound. He nodded, handed her the towel, walked to the front of the door, and opened it suddenly. She jumped around the door to take a look at what was going on, just as she heard sounds of a fight. Before she realized it, she was being pushed back out of the way, and he was hauling a young male in his arms into the motel room. His hand was over the man's mouth, but it wasn't necessary, as he was limp in Diesel's arms. He put him on the kitchen chair and said, "Don't get close to him."

She instinctively stepped back. "Is he involved in this?"

"I have no idea if he is or if he just thinks that it might be a nice place to find some booty," he said.

"Meaning wallets, purses?"

He nodded. "Add on to that list cell phones and even the clothes on your body."

"Seriously?"

"I'm not kidding," he said. "This is Manila. Everything's for sale here, but you must have goods to sell first."

She shuddered and walked back to the little kitchenette, where she poured herself a glass of water. It wasn't the cleanest-looking water, but no notice about a boil advisory was posted, and certainly no bottled water was around.

She sipped it, realized it tasted fine, and had a big glass. "What will you do with him?"

"Ask him a few questions," he said. "Don't worry. I won't beat him up."

"Good," she said cheerfully. "I really don't like the sight of blood."

"Seriously? You do stem-cell research, and you don't like the sight of blood?"

"Well, not fresh," she said, with a grin.

He just nodded. He picked up his phone, took a photo of the guy, and sent it off.

"And what'll that tell you?"

"Whether he's got a record, if he's into breaking into hotel rooms, it's hard to say. And maybe it'll tell me noth-ing." He dropped his phone nearby.

Eva said, "The problem now is, he's unconscious, so you can't ask him anything."

He looked at her, smiled, and said, "A smack across his face will wake him up."

"I doubt it," she said.

"He's more or less just trying to play dead, thinking he can make a run for the door."

At that, she walked around and looked at the young man. "He looks like he's out to me."

"Of course he does," he said. "He has to keep looking that way too."

She shrugged; he motioned her farther back. "You really think he'll jump me?"

"Well, I would," he said. "So, yeah."

She just stared at him in shock, and then, all of a sudden, the young man burst from the chair and headed for the door. And he almost made it.

But Diesel grabbed the back of his shirt, hauling him into the kitchen and slamming him back into the chair. He looked at the kid and said, "I said, sit. This time stay there." He looked at her. "Like I said, give them an inch, and they're trying to take a yard."

Just then came a knock on the door. He looked over at the kid on the chair, pointed at him, and said, "Sit." And he walked to the door and opened it.

Jerricho walked in, carrying bags of food. He stopped when he saw the kid at the table. "I didn't know we had company," he said, with that dry tone of his. "I would have brought more food." He walked to the far side of the table, put the food down, looked over at Diesel.

"Unexpected company. Unexpected and unwelcome," he murmured. "And we're not sharing our food with this kid."

"Good, so I'm just in time for the interrogation."

"Well, if the kid's smart, he'll tell us exactly what he knows, and he gets to walk out of here with all his teeth and his limbs attached."

The kid immediately stared up at him in shock. "I don't know anything." Although a bit garbled his English was clear enough to understand.

The two men just nodded. "Of course you don't. Let's say, that's how you guys work. Great, you take a few bucks to go in and check out the apartment, see what they've got, scoping around. We let you go because there's absolutely nothing too scary about you, and then you come back with your buddies."

The kid looked at him in horror.

"Right?"

He shook his head immediately. "No, of course not. I would never do something like that."

"Well," Eva said, "the alternative's much worse." She walked over so she could study him closer. "You know what? An awful lot of seasoning is in your eyes for somebody supposedly so young."

"That's common here," Diesel said. "The trouble is, I want to know who sent him and why."

"Probably for our laptops most likely," Jerricho said.

"I don't know," she said. "I think it was to kill us."

At that, the kid looked at her and jumped up immediately.

Diesel pressed him back into the chair. "I said, sit!"

"I don't have anything to do with murder," the kid yelled.

She looked at the age creases in the corner of his eyes and at the world-wearied look in his gaze, and she said, "I don't believe you." He was probably sixteen, but he looked like he was over twenty. A hard life will do that to you.

"Honest," he said, trying for an earnest look. He looked at the other two and said, "Okay, okay. I was told to come in, case the joint."

"Now that you have, what will you tell them?" Jerricho said, with a laugh. "You can tell them that the two guys caught you, so you couldn't figure out what was here. Or will you tell them that you found a laptop, cell phones, and a pretty young woman?"

At that, the kid had the grace to look ashamed. He looked over at her and said, "Sorry, it's part of the deal."

"You tell others if there's a female?" she asked in horror.

He just shrugged. "Women sell, are valuable," he said.

Her gaze went from to Diesel, back to the kid, and again to Diesel. "Is he serious?"

"He's very serious," Diesel said. "Women are a valuable commodity."

She shook her head slowly. "Please, no," she said. "I don't want to think of this place being into slave trade."

"It's not slave trade," the kid protested. "The women do what women do."

"What's that?" she asked.

He looked at her, frowned, looked over at Diesel.

Diesel smiled at him. "You should probably answer her question."

"Women. They have sex with men," he said. "That's what women do."

She sat down with a hard *thud*. "Is that all you think women do?"

"Sure," he said. "What else?"

"Wow," she said. "I don't even know where to start, but I'm a scientist for one."

At the term, he looked at her, confused. "Scientist?"

"Yes," she said in a dry tone. "I work in a lab, where I find cures for diseases. But I think the disease that you have is a lack of humanity."

He obviously didn't have a clue what she was talking about, and that just made her realize how much worse this really was. She looked over at Diesel. "Will you let him go?"

"Well, we'll have to," he said, "but not too fast. I think we'll leave him in a ditch somewhere."

He immediately jumped out of his chair, and Diesel immediately slammed him back down again.

"I don't care what you do with him," she said. "You could throw him *where men do what men do*."

At that, all three men looked at her, and Diesel asked, "What does that mean?"

"Well, if he wanted me for what *women do*," she said, "then I think you should want him to do *what men do*."

"What's that?"

With a hard voice, she said, "Shit on the world. Find a great big toilet, and dump him in it," she snapped.

The two men looked at her with serious expressions on their faces.

She rolled her eyes. "No, I'm not talking about you two," she said, "but nothing in this kid's attitude makes me want to stay here."

"Good thing we're not staying," Diesel said. He looked over at the punk. "Who's your boss?"

"I don't have one," he said immediately.

"Who you're scouting for?"

"No one."

"Too late," she said. "You already said that you were sent in. Who sent you in?"

He stared at her, looked over at the men, and just shrugged.

"That's fine. Get your team to deep-six him. He's just a waste of money. There's only so much clean air and water on this planet, and this guy doesn't deserve to have any of it." She walked to the food, opened up the bags, and sniffed. "Wow," she said, "this smells delicious."

Jerricho took the containers out of the bag. "I just brought a selection," he said, "street food mostly."

"Fine, a little street food works for me," she said.

There were no plates, but he had picked up chopsticks, so she opened up one of the containers and started in on it.

The kid looked at her and said, "I could have some food too."

"You could," she said, "but you know what? *Women do what women do*, and I'm not sharing because that's not what women do. As far as I'm concerned, you'd better shut up and get the hell out of my sight before I get really angry with you."

He stared at her. "You have no reason to be angry with me."

"How many women are you responsible for dumping into a brothel?"

"Well, some we hire out," he said, with a shrug, "after we use them ourselves."

"Jesus," she said.

Diesel looked at the kid and said, "You better shut up right there. The Western world doesn't appreciate rapists and sex traffickers."

The kid looked at him and said, "In Manila, it happens all the time."

"But that doesn't mean it *should* happen," she snapped. "That doesn't mean the women are willing."

"Doesn't matter if they are not," he said, almost bewildered. "It's the way the world works."

"Here maybe," she said, tossing down the chopsticks, suddenly her appetite no longer existed. "But it shouldn't."

And she stood, walked to the bathroom, and closed the door. She stared at herself in the mirror, knowing that sex trafficking of women and children had happened the world over, but to think that this guy admitted to it, and knowing that the police system was so bad right now that it probably wouldn't do any good to call the cops on him, she sat here for a long moment, wishing she was anywhere but here.

When a gentle knock came on the door, she called out, "Come in." The door opened, and Diesel, standing there, leaned against the doorjamb. "Are you okay?"

She shrugged. "It's a cesspool of humanity out there," she said. "I really don't want to be touched by it any more than I have to."

"He is part of a bigger issue here."

"Which is why I doubt there's any point in calling the cops on him, is there?"

"I didn't say that," he said. "I think we'll turn him over to one of my teams, and they can collect the entire gang, see how far the roots of this go. It will only be one of the Hydra's heads, but it would be something."

She looked at him gratefully. "Do you think they'd help?" she cried out. "Just to think of all these young women thrown into their sex-for-hire system is enough to make me puke."

"Well, he's out cold right now because I got tired of listening to him talk," he said. "Come on out and finish eating."

She looked at him and shook her head. "My stomach's not very happy."

"Well, we'll be leaving soon," he said, "so I need to make sure that you have a nap and that you have food."

She groaned, as she got up from the edge of the bathtub, where she'd been seated, and walked back out again. Happily, she realized the idiot was tied up and unconscious. "I'd really appreciate it if you'd keep him that way until we leave."

"Won't have to worry about it," Jerricho said, as he tapped his cell phone. "He's getting picked up within the hour."

She looked at him gratefully. "Good. Because the last thing I want to happen is him opening his mouth again."

"Third-world countries have a very different system."

"But it's still the same, isn't it?" she said passionately. "Women are at the bottom of the list, treated like nothing more than chattel. Used and abused and tossed to the side when no longer wanted. I wanted to be a lawyer for the longest time as well, particularly being in law enforcement. It just always felt like nobody cared. *I do.*"

"It's not always like that," he said. "It's just, right now, with everything else going on, you're feeling very victimized."

"Yeah, you could say that," she said. She picked up one of the food containers, opened it, and had several more bites, before putting it down.

"You haven't eaten at all."

"I will soon."

He checked his watch, and then a buzz came on his phone. He pulled it out, checked it, and nodded. He walked to the door and waited for a rap three times. He opened it up, and four men walked in, took one look, and the kid was quickly lifted and carried out, and, just like that, they were gone. She slowly put her hand to her heart. She looked over at Diesel. "You can't just kill him, can you?"

"They won't kill him. But they will find out who's on the rest of his team, so they can stop what they're doing. The cops here aren't too bad, since the new president took over. He's a hard-ass, and he's got rules that most of the Western world wouldn't agree with, but he doesn't have any truck with these crimes either."

She nodded slowly. "Well, I'm just glad the kid's gone," she said.

"And our flights have been moved up, so that's good. I was afraid we wouldn't get out until tomorrow."

"Good, I can't wait to be back in the US."

"Except we're heading to Australia first."

She stopped, thought about it, nodded, and said, "That makes sense. And I don't really care. That's one step closer to home, and it's a good place to be too."

"Exactly," he said. "We have to be at the airport in two hours. Before you know it, we'll be at the airport, taking off."

"You still expect it to be dangerous?" she asked.

"It's not that we expect it to be dangerous," he said, "but we're always keeping an eye out for danger."

"Right," she said. "A small but significant difference."

"Very significant," he said. "What you're really asking is, do we have any intel that tells us if we're still in danger. And the answer is, no, we don't, but, because of what happened to Marge, we can't ever rest. Not until we get you home."

She smiled, nodded, and said, "Thank you." And, with that, she looked at her food and said, "I really can't do much more damage to this."

"Go rest," he said. "The food will still be here when you wake up."

"Fine." She rose, and, as she went past him, she stopped, looked up, smiled, and said, "Thank you again."

He just chuckled, gave her a hug, and said, "Go lie down."

And, with that, she headed to the bed. She turned her back to them, as she laid down on the bed, stretched out fully, and closed her eyes. And, if nothing else, it was just nice to know that she was safe.

Even as she closed her eyes, her thoughts still horrified her. Just coming out of captivity, the thought of going into another was mind-boggling. And the punk had said it so casually, as if it made absolutely no difference to him what happened to the women around him. Didn't he have mothers, daughters, or sisters? She hoped that one day he learned the value of females. Even if only as a very best friend.

The world needed to change. She just didn't think it would happen fast enough for her liking. At that last thought she pulled her knees up higher, punched the pillow under her, and closed her eyes to help fall asleep. If she were lucky, she'd wake up, and they'd be at the airport, already heading for the security clearance. And finally, with that drifting through her mind, she smiled ever-so-slightly and let herself sink under the waves of sleep.

DIESEL CHECKED IN on Eva, but she was sleeping soundly. He walked back to Jerricho. "I don't like anything about this."

"Do you want to move?"

Diesel stood, thinking for three seconds, and then nodded. "I absolutely do."

Surprised, Jerricho looked at him. "Do you think the kid's really connected?"

"No," he said, "but anything that brings attention to us is bad news."

"Yes, I agree with you there," he said. "We can get another safe place."

"We're supposed to be flying out though," he murmured.

"Let me check in to make sure everything's running fine." Two seconds later Jerricho looked up and shook his head. "No," he said, "it's not."

"What's not?"

"The Manila airport's been temporarily shut down."

"Shit!" he said. "Seriously?"

"Yes."

They stared at each other, both trying to figure out whether it was connected to them or not. In the end, Diesel shook his head and said, "We can't take a chance."

"I agree," he said.

"If the airport is shut down, we could do a small plane, seaplane, or we end up taking a ship out." He said, "Other than that, we don't have too many options. We should have gone in the other direction. Shit! Shit! Shit!"

"Don't go there," Jerricho said. "We can deal with this."

"I don't want to fly back to China, and I don't want to go in any other direction except toward North America."

"We might have to backtrack in order to go forward."

"Let's see what our options are." He sat down and checked the airport and agreed. Everything was shut down temporarily. "And there's no sign of when it'll reopen," he murmured.

"Of course not. And then we have the additional problem that we don't know what security measures they'll have in place, as soon as it does open."

"You're not saying anything I don't already know," Diesel said. "Who's in the ocean around here?"

"Thinking US Navy again?"

"Or private yacht again?" he said. "We can get a helicopter, and we could probably hire a floatplane. But our distance gained will be fairly short for each."

"We can go to one of the other islands."

Diesel nodded slowly. It took them an hour, and he looked at their options and said, "I think that might be our best bet."

"There is a base."

"I know. I was thinking of that," he said. "If we can get to the base, then we could get out to the ocean again."

"And then what?" Jerricho asked.

"We'll have to take the ship, whichever direction it's going," he said. "And it doesn't really matter, it's all about keeping her safe. We're not in a rush."

"Agreed. Australia is our best bet," he said. "It might take us a couple trips, but that still looks to be the better end result."

"We'll fit in better, and we should have more options for international flights," Diesel said.

"Do you want to let the Australian government know?"

Diesel thought about it for a long moment and shook his head. "As much as I'd like them on our side, if we should run into trouble, the fewer people who know, the better."

"I got no problem with that," Jerricho said. He sat down. "You want to talk to Shane or shall I?"

"I will." He quickly opened the chat and sent a message, looking for passage to Australia. At that, a question mark came back. He just shook his head. **Don't ask me any questions. Just do it.**

He gave a brief explanation, but basically it boiled down to his instincts saying this was a bad deal, and they needed to move, and they needed to move now. As soon as he heard the airport was closed, it was a done deal as far as he was concerned.

Shane agreed. He came back less than eight minutes later. **Rendezvous at this dock, this town, within forty-eight minutes.**

He swore when he looked at it. "Forty-eight minutes? Not much time." He sent a message saying, **We need a ride.**

It'll be at your door in seven.

He bolted to his feet, quickly packed up what they had unpacked, ditched the food, and looked in the direction of the bed. He glanced back at Jerricho. "She won't like this."

"Doesn't matter what she likes," he said quietly. "It keeps her alive, and it keeps her safe."

On that note, his bag at the front door, Diesel walked up to her bed and gently reached out a hand to wake her up.

When she opened her sleepy eyes, he smiled at her and said, "We have to go."

She blinked several times, got up soundlessly, threw on her dirty jeans, slipped into her flip-fops, and followed him. He didn't know if it was her time in captivity, but she was almost too acquiescent for his liking.

Jerricho didn't say a word as she followed Diesel out. But he was surprised when she didn't say anything. "Eva, are you okay?"

She blinked several times, reached up to her temple, and said, "I don't even know what time it is, but I'm trusting you."

He quickly opened the door, and, with a motion to stay quiet, they slipped down the back way, and outside she took several long slow deep breaths of the still sticky air. "Where are we going? It's not time for our flight yet."

"No," Diesel said, "change of plans."

At that, she stopped and looked at him and said, "Oh. I guess I really wasn't awake when you woke me up."

"That's okay," he said. "Keep doing what you're doing."

"You mean, follow blindly?"

"Yes, and stay quiet." At that, she immediately clammed up. And he ushered her around to the front, and there was the car. He put her into the back seat and took the wheel.

She leaned forward and said to Jerricho, in the passenger seat, "Do you know what we're doing?"

He grinned and nodded. "I do."

"Good," she said. "Glad somebody does. How long will we be?"

"We have to be at our destination in thirty-five minutes," Jerricho said.

She stared at him. "Or else?"

"Or else we miss it."

With that, she took another calming breath and said, "I'll curl up in the back seat. You let me know if we make it or not."

Diesel gave a bark of laughter, and she dropped her head on her arms, as he sped through the city streets. He looked over at Jerricho. "Nice to be so innocent in life, huh?"

Jerricho looked around, saw she was apparently sleeping again, and said, "On the other hand, this is the easiest thing for us."

They needed to get to their destination fast, but he also needed to make sure he didn't attract any attention, so he didn't want to be too early, yet he didn't want to be late. He needed to be just on time, and he needed to make sure that everything was moving at the same time. By the time they pulled up to their destination, they were a whole two minutes early.

He pulled up alongside the wharf, turned off the engine, reached around to the back, grasped Eva's hip, and gave her a gentle push. She murmured gently. He said, "Wake up. We're here."

At that, her eyes opened wide, and she stared at him blankly.

Then she sat up slowly, yawned, and said, "I don't know where *here* is," she said, "but let's go." She stepped out of the vehicle. He quickly ushered her around to his side and down to the water. A small fishing boat was there that looked like it had seen much better days, but, as long as it was seaworthy, he didn't care. She looked at him doubtfully, as they got close enough, and he just shook his head and ushered her on board.

"How can you be sure it's the one you're waiting for?" she asked. "It's not like anybody's here to sign you on or sign you off or anything like that."

"It's fine," he said.

She rolled her eyes. "For all I know, you're stealing it."

Jerricho chuckled quietly and said, "Nope, it's all good." He quickly helped her onboard.

And, with that, Diesel untied from the wharf, hopped into the front, and then gently pushed away from shore.

She watched as they used the long-handled poles to move from the sandy shore. "Looks like you've done this a time or two."

"A time or two," he said quietly. He looked over at her, smiled, and said, "How was your nap?"

"Not long enough apparently," she said, "because this still doesn't make much sense."

"Do you always sleep until it makes sense?"

"Somewhat, yes," she said, yawning. "How long will we

be here?"

"Long enough, if you want to close your eyes again," Jerricho murmured.

She shook her head. "This is a unique experience. I'm okay to sit here and to enjoy it for a bit." And then a question popped out. "Why aren't we at the airport?"

"It's closed temporarily," Diesel said from up front. At that Jerricho stepped forward and pointed out something in the distance. "We decided it was time to change plans." Diesel sat down beside her, as Jerricho started the outboard motor. Diesel looked at her intently. "Are you okay?"

"I'm okay," she said. "A little confused but willing to keep going."

"I get that you trust me because you don't have much else for options," he said, "but we really do need you to trust us so, when we tell you to do something, so we know that you'll do it."

"Have I not yet so far?" she asked.

CHAPTER 11

EVA WAS AWAKE now at least. It seemed like she had been woken and slept, and woken and slept, and it was just this bad dream. As she sat here, she felt the wind pick up. Instantly Diesel wrapped an arm around her and tucked her up close.

She looked up at him and smiled. "You seem to be doing that a lot."

"What?"

"Hugging me."

"Just trying to protect you from the wind."

"Maybe," she said, "but I like it anyway."

He burst out chuckling. "Glad to hear that."

She smiled. "Of course, if it's just a work thing, then maybe that should be a different issue altogether."

"In what way?" he asked, tightening his arms and shifting his position.

She snuggled in, as the wind picked up. "How much farther do we have to go?" she asked, changing the subject.

"We're heading out to that black speck," he said, pointing.

She shivered. "That'll mean I'll get colder."

"I'm here," he said. "Just lean against me."

She smiled. "That's what I mean. You're always looking after my comforts."

"I'm trying to keep you safe," he said.

She nodded, her body instinctively stiffening slightly.

"Did I say something wrong?" he asked, his low tone against her ear.

"No," she said, "not at all. I just have to remember that you're only here to help me out."

"And is there another reason that you would want me to be here?"

That was a leading question if there ever was one. She thought about it and nodded. "Well, I like you," she said, "but I don't know anything about you."

"What do you want to know?" he said. "I'm an open book."

She laughed at that. "No," she said, "you're dark and mysterious."

He burst out chuckling again. "I'm so not."

She smiled. "I appreciate what you've done for me."

"Yep, ease up on the gratitude," he said. "I wouldn't want you to confuse that with anything else."

She twisted in his arms, feeling the shivers as a new body part was exposed to the wind. "And what does that mean?"

His gaze was inscrutable. But he answered readily enough. "One of the things that we have to watch out for," he said, "is gratitude being mistaken for something else."

She thought about that for a long moment. "As if I would become infatuated, thinking that you were some big hero in a romance book?"

"Something like that," he said.

She thought about it and nodded. "I can see how that could be an issue. At least for some people. We're just so grateful that it's easy to see you in another light. I, of course, know that you can be difficult, unmanageable, and obtuse at times."

He burst out laughing yet again. "All of that?" he asked. "Really?"

"Absolutely," she said with a smile.

"Well, I'm glad you're perfect."

"No," she said, "I'm not at all. And I certainly am not mistaking the interest we have here."

He was silent for a moment, and then he squeezed her gently and said, "Good, I'm glad to hear that."

She smiled at that. "Glad we got some of the preliminaries out of the way."

"Is that what we're doing?" he asked curiously.

"I'm not sure," she said. "I honestly haven't done much dating lately, so I feel very out of practice."

"*Hmm*," he said. "Honesty works best for me."

"You and me both," she said, nodding. "I much prefer a straightforward conversation and assessment. I always hated that dancing around in a relationship, trying to figure out what the other person really felt."

"Ditto," he said, shifting once more.

She immediately twisted and asked, "Am I too heavy?"

"There's nothing to you, so, no, you're not too heavy."

"There's lots to me," she said, protesting.

He shook his head, reached out, and pulled her back up against him. "Snuggle up. I don't want you to catch a chill," he said.

She snuggled into his warmth. "I love how warm you are. It's like lying against a furnace."

"It's normal for me," he said.

"It's amazing," she whispered, as she curled up a little closer. His arms wrapped around her, gently shifting her, so that she was a little more comfortable too. She just smiled, noting that, once again, it was all about her comfort and not his. "But then again," she said, "I didn't even ask. Maybe you have a relationship ongoing."

"Nope," he said cheerfully. "Single." And then he stopped and asked, "What about you?"

She caught an odd tone in his voice. She twisted to look up at him and smiled. "Nope, and I come from the belief that I'm with one person at a time," she said. "I know it's an unusual attitude in today's day and age."

"Not for me. I'm the same." He just smiled at that. "Maybe because I'm a bit of a dinosaur when it comes to relationships."

"Good," she said. And then, she chuckled. "You do realize that we're just getting the basics out of the way. So that we have a good idea who and what we are."

"Danger also accelerates relationships," he said. "You really get to know who people are when the stakes are high."

"How does that work?" she asked.

"Well, think about it," he said. "If you do the dating scene, you can take months and months before seeing what somebody will be like under stress and under pressure. In something like this, we see that person show up immediately."

"So, if I was weeping and wailing and crying?" she asked. "You'd know something about me that you wouldn't normally see?"

"To a certain extent, yes. Because, if you were dating, how long would it be before you actually saw something like that?"

She nodded. "Right. So now what does my behavior tell you?"

"That you're steady. That you can handle rough, high-stress situations. You can follow orders, when orders are snapped out because they're necessary. You're accommodating, and you pivot quickly."

She thought about that assessment and nodded slowly. "You know what? I think you're right with that. I hadn't really considered it. But is that of any value?"

"It's of huge value. You're not a whiner. You're not somebody who'll complain because you didn't have your fancy clothing or the special food you wanted or the coffee that you must have. You can share a bed and a bathroom. You didn't need to have your own room," he said. "You know what? A lot of people have very heavy diva traits, and we deal with those people because they're part and parcel of the job we do, but that doesn't mean a diva is anybody I would choose to be with. I know it works for a lot of people and great for them." He added, "It's not necessarily my preferred personality."

"Mine either," she said. "I can't stand working with them either."

"Exactly." At that, she snuggled back in again. "So I have a question for you," he said.

She once again twisted to look up at him.

"You're getting a kink in your neck," he said. And he lifted her up and pivoted her sideways, so she sat between his legs, with her legs hooked over his thigh.

And she now faced him, her arm around his back. "What is it?"

"Where do you live? How do you live? And what are you doing when this is over?"

DIESEL LOVED THE way Eva burst out laughing in delight. He grinned. "So bad questions or good questions?"

"They were the right questions," she admitted. "And honestly I'm not exactly sure what I'm doing, but I would like to see you again."

"Good. Even if I'm not out rescuing you?"

"Oh, Lord," she said, "please, let me be in a scenario where I don't need to be rescued ever again."

"Hear! Hear! For that. Are you likely to be in trouble again after this?"

"I hope not," she said. "I think I'll change jobs though."

"Are you blaming the lab?"

"I'm not so much blaming the lab as much as I'm wondering if it was their lax security that got me in trouble or their need to have press releases, showing their progress. I get that we must have investors, but, at what point in time, is it dangerous for the staff?"

"Do you think there's any connection to why you were targeted?"

"Well, I have to consider it," she said. "I don't like to, but I do have to."

"And?"

"It's inconclusive," she said. "My work was handed over. Everybody at the company who's working on the same project has access to the same information, the same conclusions I do. I don't know where the Chinese would have gotten the information that we had, what we had, but I know that the media had really made a big deal out of some of our research findings, and that was good in the sense that the company needed the influx of cash that came from that. But it was dangerous," she said, "and, apparently because of it, we were most likely targeted. So do I want to work for a company where having investor money outweighs the risk? No."

"But did they know what the risk was?"

"I don't know," she said quietly. "Again that's part of that trust that I'll have to reexamine."

"Well, take some time with your father and see how you feel about the job afterward. You love your work, don't you?"

"I really do," she said with a smile. "But then I have to question whether I love it because it was the challenge and maybe more challenges are out there for me or whether it's time for a change. I don't know. This scenario has made me rethink a whole lot in life."

"Such as?"

She looked up at him. "For you, this is normal. You get into these situations that are rife with danger, and you know how to get yourself out of it. For me, this is one of those eye-opening *I didn't know if I would live or die* scenarios," she said. "I still don't know really. I mean, if you think about it, we're still on the path to get me back safely. And then I have to question, is this the kind of work I want to do? Is this … I mean, if you were told that you had forty days left to live, what would you choose to do with those forty days?"

He stared at her in surprise.

She shrugged. "This is just some of what was rolling around my head the entire time that I was a captive. The things that are important before you lose your freedom are something that you have to reexamine when you do regain that freedom. What's important to me? It was my father," she said. "While my brother is part of the family too, my father is the only person I know who loves me for me and who I love unequivocally. So now what I really want is to spend time with him. Maybe when this danger, … when this panic is over, I'll feel differently about that. I don't know. But all I can think about is getting back to the people who care about me, so I can have that special hug again."

"I don't think there's anything wrong with that," Diesel said quietly. "It's one of the reasons that we do what we do. It's to bring people home."

She nodded. "That's a big thing. *Home*. What does home mean to me? And it means different things now. Back then when I, … before this captivity—and I guess I'll have a life that's *before* and a life that's *after* now—but before captivity, *home* was just that place that I lived in. My work was my life. It was my passion." She said, "But now …" And then she stopped.

He looked at her, gently squeezed her, and asked, "And now?"

"I'm not so sure," she said, her voice changing. "Watching Paul die, knowing that Marge is gone …" She closed her mouth and burrowed in closer.

He felt the shaking of her shoulders, and he just held her. "Now you get another chance," he said quietly. "You get to reassess what it is you want for your life now. It's not a case of having missed out, … having made a mistake. It's not a case of having been in the wrong place at the wrong time. It's a chance right now to redo what you were doing. And decide again, is this what you want? And, if it isn't what you want, you get to change it."

"Is it that simple?" she whispered.

"I think it can be," he said, with a nod. "I mean, a lot of people have multiple careers. A lot of people work from home. Maybe you would feel better doing that."

"I'm not sure I could," she said, "just because of the kind

of work I do."

"And that's another question. Is that the work you want to continue doing? Do you want a family?"

"I didn't," she said, "until I lost the ability to choose that future for myself. But now? ... And now maybe I do. I hadn't really assessed it that way. I hadn't looked at it. I just knew that everything that I could have was out in the future, and I guess that's what the real problem is," she said, as if trying to work her way forward. "I was working, burying myself in my work. I always thought there was time for all this other stuff later. You know? The husband, the two kids, the home with the white picket fence," she said with a gentle smile.

"And there still is time," he said. "You're what? Knocking on thirty?"

"Almost," she said. "And even just saying that now makes me more aware of my biological clock.

"But women are having babies a lot later in life."

"Absolutely they are, but I'm not sure having children later in my life is what I want," she said. "Say I do have them at forty, between forty and forty-five. Do I want to be between sixty and sixty-five with a twenty-year-old?" she asked. "But the point that I'm getting at is, when they took away my freedom, they took away those down-the-road future possibilities, and I suddenly realized that I hadn't had that joy of giving birth or even the joy of marriage. I've never met that one person I wanted to go that distance with, and, because of that captivity, it's as if all of that was taken away from me."

"And you haven't had a chance to assess where you're at now, right? You're still thinking you're a captive?"

"I know I'm not a captive," she said earnestly. "I get

that. I really do. But the captive mentality? … I haven't shaken it off yet. Maybe that's what I'm trying to say." But enough doubt remained in her voice that she looked up at him, shrugged, and said, "I'm not explaining it very well."

"I think you did very well," he said. "The truth of the matter is, you've had your world shaken up, and now you'll take another look at your priorities. If you were to die or were to know that you had only forty days left, what would you do? It's not long enough to have a child, no matter how strong your medicine is."

She burst out laughing at that. "No," she said, "it isn't. And I wouldn't want to bring a child into this world, knowing that I'm not there to raise it. At the same time, you know the only thing that really matters is those I love." She added, "The money doesn't replace those people I love. The job doesn't. Not even the passion for the work I do. It really doesn't right now. If I only had forty days, I'd go to the lake and spend it all with my dad."

"And I can really appreciate that," he murmured. "In fact," he smiled, "I think I'd probably do the same thing."

She looked up at him in astonishment. "I figured you'd tell me to go travel the world and do something memorable."

"I think when we know that our time is coming or that we know that there's an end near, all we really want to do is be with the people we want to be with," he said. "And, in this case, that's your father. I understand that completely."

She smiled. "Thank you."

"No," he said, "don't be so hard on yourself. There's nothing wrong with wanting to spend time with your father."

"Outside of my forty-days-to-live theory, doesn't mean I want to stay there long though," she said, laughing. "We do get along, but I get sick of fishing."

He grinned. "I love to fish," he said, "but I don't know how long something like that would work for me."

"Well, I tell you what. Why don't you come fishing with me?" she asked impulsively. "You'll take some of the stress off."

He burst out laughing. "So what you're actually saying is," he murmured, "that you would prefer if I came, so you don't have to go fishing."

"I really do enjoy it," she said. "I'm just not nuts about it."

He grinned. "Well, I'm not either, but it would be nice to get back out on the lake."

"Good," she said, "it's a date."

"If you say so," he said. "Maybe you want to check with your father first."

"Nope," she said, "he'll be delighted." She gazed at him thoughtfully. "Honestly he'll be really delighted. So will my brother."

"Ah, don't tell me. He's trying to make sure that you're taken care of."

"I think he'd be happy if I wasn't alone, put it that way."

"And how do you feel about that?"

"Well, when I was having all those lovely thoughts about having lost my future, as I had hoped it to be," she said, "I had to wonder again if he wasn't right. Being alone like that, it's not the most comfortable place to be in your life."

"No, it isn't," he said, "but I don't know that we can force a relationship to occur, just because we're ready for it."

"No, I don't think so, but I don't want to force anything either. I'd like to think it would happen naturally."

"And it probably would," he said. "I think it's just about

giving it time. Maybe now that your focus won't be quite so heavily on your job, maybe there'll be room for other things."

She nodded. "I think I agree with that." She twisted to look across the ocean.

He murmured, "Still hours yet."

"Are you taking over the driving of the boat?" she asked, pointing up at Jerricho.

He shook his head. "No, Jerricho really loves this," he said, "so I'm on babysitting duty." But he said it with such a gentle chuckle that he hoped that she didn't take offense.

She sank back against him. "He seems nice," she said, "but I don't feel the same connection with him."

"Good," he said. "He is really nice. He's a good guy, and he'll be there and look after you every step of the way." He added, "And, if anything happens to me, you listen to him. Do you hear me?"

She looked up at him in horror. He shook his head and placed a finger across her lips and said, "I'm not saying something will, but, in this job, we never know, and I want to make sure that you do follow what he tells you to do. Got it?"

She wrinkled up her nose. "I got it, but I don't like it."

"You don't have to like it," he said smoothly, "you just have to listen to me."

"Okay, fine," she said. Then she shot him a look. "You know something? For somebody who doesn't handle a whole lot of change, this has already been enough for me. I'd like a nice clean, safe ride home."

"And we'll get it," he said, "but now it's a little bit more of an up-and-down journey."

"Fast?"

"No, we took speed, … the requirement for speed, out of it," he said, "once we realized that the airport was closed."

"Do you think that was connected to us?"

"I don't know," he said. "It might have been absolutely nothing at all, but it was that little instinctive warning system of mine that wouldn't let me forget it."

"Well, I'm okay to be here right now," she said. She opened her mouth and yawned.

"Sleep if you can," he urged. "It'll be a long couple days."

She winced. "I was actually hoping to have food."

"Not yet," he said, "when we get to the ship."

"Okay," she said, "maybe I'll try to sleep." And she snuggled in deeper.

Diesel shifted, so he could lean back in place, tucked her up a little closer, wrapped his open jacket around her to keep her back from the wind a bit, and just held her. It wasn't long before her slow even breathing was obvious. He looked up to see Jerricho watching him.

Jerricho nodded at the sleeping beauty in his arms. "How's she doing?"

"She's better," he said. "A little rattled, a little nervous, still dealing with the kidnapping and the scenarios that could have gone wrong. But she's working on it."

"It's hard, isn't it?" he said. "Every time we deal with somebody saved in these missions, the issues are slightly different, yet, in some ways, they're all the same."

"Well, it's a shock and a loss of innocence that every-body has to deal with, one way or another," he murmured. He kept his voice low to ensure she couldn't hear him.

"You two seem to be getting along just fine." Of course Jerricho's grin was wide and wolfish.

"We are," Diesel said in a neutral voice.

"I told you."

"Not too interested in hearing that *you told me so*," he said.

"Well, I still think I'm right."

"Maybe, but we are not going there right now."

"That works for me too," Jerricho said. "I'm not seeing any boogeyman around this corner," he said, "so that's a good trip so far."

"Let's hope we don't have any. We made enough preparations to slide out quietly."

"Doesn't mean that somebody didn't see our vehicle as we pulled up to the boat."

"The team should have picked up our vehicle by now," Diesel said.

"I'm sure it was," he said. "It still doesn't change the fact that somebody could have seen us park and get on board."

"That's possible. We don't … she doesn't have any tracking on her, right?"

"The navy checked for it on the destroyer," he said, "and nothing was found."

"The question is whether the Chinese have a technology that we don't know how to track."

"I was thinking of that too," he said. "But, if she ingested something or was injected with something, the farther away we get, it should be more difficult to track her."

"Agreed, and we are quite a distance now from Shanghai."

"It would still be easier if we knew."

"But how to find out?" he said.

"That's always the problem, isn't it? How long ago was it planted? How many days now?" he said. "It should have passed through her system, if she'd eaten it, swallowed it."

"And I don't think she was given anything like that."

"Not to mention they took out the other two scientists. How did they know?"

"Paul could have just been a simple case of being followed. It's one of the reasons that we chose to get out of the lab as fast as we could, right?"

"I know," he said.

"But Marge?"

"Exactly. I just … It's niggling in the back of my mind."

"Mine too," he said. "I just wish there were a way to figure out if Eva had been given something."

"Do you have a magnet around?" he asked.

"No, I don't. Do you?" They both shook their heads.

At that, she opened her eyes and stared up at them. "What would a magnet tell you?"

"Possibly nothing," he said. "Just wondering if a piece of metal were embedded in your skin, and, if you, … if we're being tracked."

"God, that would be too much." She stopped to think and said, "When I first woke up there, at the Chinese lab, I had pain at the back to my neck," she said, reaching up under her hair.

He immediately tilted her head forward and took a look. Found an ever-so-slight lump on the side. "Do you know how long it bothered you?"

"No, more like just an irritant, like a bite."

He looked over at Jerricho. "You need to take a look at this." He sat her up and said, "Let Jerricho look."

Jerricho walked over, and Diesel quickly hopped up and took over the piloting of the boat. Jerricho returned a moment later and nodded. "I'd take it out. If for no other reason that the military couldn't find it on the ship, which means it's new tech. Likely a prototype. So, if we have it, we can analyze it and combat it, before they start widespread use."

"Great," he said. He walked back over, sat down, almost falling down at the uneven waves.

She looked at him worriedly, having heard their conversation.

"We have to be sure," he said.

She swallowed hard and then nodded.

"See? That's what I mean," he said. "You've got grit, and you know what needs to be done, and you'll let me do it."

"Do I have a choice?" she said, her tone dry.

"No," he said, "you really don't." He pulled a pocketknife from his boot.

She looked at it and sighed. "It'd be nice if you could at least sterilize it."

He dipped it into the ocean. "If nothing else, it's saltwater, and I know it'll sting, but it won't sting badly because I'll make a very surface-level cut."

"Fine," she said. She leaned forward, until she was right over him, her head lying on his thigh. "Go for it," she muttered.

He took one look, gently stretched out the skin, taut over the top of the small lump, and, with a clean slice, cut through it. She gasped, and he said, "I've already sliced."

"Good," she said. "Can you get it out?"

"Just stay still for a moment," he said. And, using the tip of the knife, he dug ever-so-slightly and finally pulled out what looked like a tiny little ball, like a shot pellet. He looked at it, frowned, and then put it underneath her face, so that she saw it.

"What is that?" she asked.

"I'm afraid it might have been tracking," he said. "It's definitely something man-made, and I presume you didn't put it in there."

"No," she said. She reached up a hand, and he pulled her hand down.

"Just leave it. It needs to heal now. We don't want your dirty fingers on it."

She wrinkled up her face. "Well, a bandage would be nice."

"Not happening," he said, "at least not until we get to the ship."

She nodded, and he watched as a little drop of blood slowly worked its way down her neck. She reached up and wiped it clear.

He said, "When we get to the ship, we'll get it washed up properly."

"Fine," she said, but she was still staring at the object in his hand. "It's so tiny. Looks like pus from a pimple." She shook her head. "Do you think they did that when I first arrived?"

"You tell me. How long ago was it that you noticed it?"

"I think right away," she said. "I just didn't think about it afterward."

"There was no need to," he said. "For all I know, there's a poison in it, and they can activate it and kill you before you actually get too far. But there's no metal in it. I'm not sure what it's made of. It was buried in your hairline and didn't show up on any of the devices you were checked with. Even the navy's top-of-the-line techno gear."

She swallowed hard, as she stared at him. "That's a little disconcerting too."

"Terrorists, bioterrorists, all of this is terrifying," he

murmured, slowly wrapping up the tiny item in a tissue before stuffing it into his pocket. "That's why we're trying to rescue you."

She nodded. "Well, I'm glad you found it, even if it's a day late."

"The farther away we are," he said, "the less chance that they could have used it for anything."

"Well, I guess that's a little more reassuring," she said. She settled back down and reached up, scrubbed her face, and asked, "How much longer?"

"About an hour," Diesel said. "Do you want to try to sleep again?"

She shook her head and then winced. "No," she said. "Finding that just reminds me of what they did to me when I wasn't awake."

"Of which you don't know that they did anything other than this," he said in a firm voice.

She shot him a look.

He shook his head. "I'm serious. Don't go worrying about a bigger issue than we can deal with right now."

"I guess," she said quietly. "It's still disconcerting."

"Very," he murmured. "Just relax."

She smiled. "If only it were that easy."

"I know, right? It's like telling somebody who's injured to just stop the pain. And, of course, it's not something anybody can do," he said. "I get that, but the bottom line is, you're safe right now, and no technology in the world could have tracked this to where we are."

"So this was just a safekeeping measure?"

"That's exactly what it was," he said.

She nodded. "Good. At least there's that reassurance."

"Absolutely," he said. "Just stay calm, and let's get to that ship. We can clean out your wound, and you'll be fine."

CHAPTER 12

DIESEL WAS RIGHT. By the time they finally made it on board—what looked like a private yacht—and Eva was taken to the bathroom, where she had the wound cleaned and just a small little bandage put on it, she felt much better about the whole deal. She also got clean clothes and a hot shower, and, as she stepped out into the galley, she was escorted to a small dining room. As she took her seat at the table, right beside an empty chair, she looked over at Jerricho. "Where's Diesel?"

"Having a shower," Jerricho said. "You want a glass of wine?"

She looked at him in surprise. "We have wine?"

He chuckled. "Absolutely," he said. "We don't have to live like heathens just because we're on the run, so to speak."

"Well, that's reassuring," she said. She picked up her wineglass as she noticed a bottle in a big cooler. "Thank you." He poured a glass for her. "What about Diesel? Will he have one?"

"He might. He might want something stronger."

"Are we allowed something stronger?" she asked curiously. "Are we on the run again?"

"Something stronger? Sure. On the run? I'm sure we will be again," he said cheerfully. "But that doesn't mean that we'll be for the next couple hours."

"Right," she nodded. "I wasn't expecting you guys to drink on the job."

"Normally I wouldn't," he said, as he sniffed the aroma of the wine, "but I do like a good glass of wine. And one glass will never hurt."

"Agreed." She picked up hers, clinked it together with his, and said, "Thank you. I don't think I've actually thanked you. I have thanked Diesel many a time, but either you're never quite around or I'm not thinking with my clear mind at the time."

"It's all right," Jerricho said, "and you're welcome."

She smiled. "This is quite the job you guys have."

"You don't know the half of it," he said, chuckling. "It's not a job that most people are used to, but we're uniquely qualified for it."

"Well, I certainly wouldn't want to do this too often," she said.

"Maybe not, but, when you see just how helpful we are in the world and how necessary this service is, you can understand."

"Yeah, I've got a question about that," she said. "How are you paid?"

"I didn't ask for particulars. In your case," he said, "we're given a job, and we do the job. Money is never brought into it."

"Well, it would be nice to think the world operates that way," she said, "but I don't think it does."

"Well, some of it does," Jerricho said. "Sometimes the world's a nice easy place to be."

"Not always," she said. "It seems to me that more people are after money than actually handing it out."

"Very true." He swirled his wine and looked down at the

glass and the beautiful red liquid in it and said, "You and Diesel seem to be getting along pretty well."

"We really are," she said, "and that is a huge surprise. I haven't had a relationship in quite a while. Haven't been too bothered, buried myself in work. I didn't find anybody I liked, and then, out of all this, he's there."

"Good," Jerricho said, "because Diesel's in a similar scenario. It's too easy to bury yourself in work and to forget about the fact that other parts of life are worth living."

"What about you?" she asked. "Are you married?"

"Not right now," he said. "I was." He smiled and added, "I really liked being married, and I would certainly sign up for it again, if I found another woman who I cared for just as much."

"What happened?"

"We married at eighteen," he said, with a wry smile. "We were just kids. A kid in love with another kid. We couldn't wait to be married, couldn't wait to be together permanently, but we couldn't make it last."

"I'm sorry," she said. "That's sad."

"It is. I went into the military after that," he said, "more as a way to stay occupied and to bury all the pain of the relationship."

"Do you still have any contact with her?"

"No, I haven't had any contact in a long time," he said. "Why?"

"Because it still seems like you're affected."

"She was my first love," he said, the corner of his lips kicking up. "We should be affected. We should always remember."

"I like that," she said, "and I think you're right. I just think so much of the world misses the point on a lot of it."

"I agree with you," he said. "That doesn't mean that it's the same for me."

"If you met her again, would you be interested?"

"I don't know," he said. "I've never had a chance to meet her again."

"Why is that?"

"Because the last time I heard, she was getting married."

"Ah!" she said. "That makes it a little different. And were you upset?"

"Upset in the sense that we hadn't made it work because I really like who she is," he said, with a nod, "but not upset that she was getting married. I wanted her to be happy."

"Yes, but usually, when people say that, they want you to be happy with them," she murmured.

"Oh, very smart," he said, lifting his glass at her. "That's very true, but it wasn't to be."

"Unless she's no longer married," she said.

"Maybe, but again that would mean a whole different mind-set for her now."

"Aah," she said, "and, therefore, maybe not one you're interested in?"

"No," he said. "Where she's been and what she's done in the meantime wouldn't have any impact." He gave a one-arm shrug. "The same for myself, but we're very different people than we were back then."

"But maybe that's a good thing," she said, with an eyebrow up. "I mean, if you really loved each other back then, and couldn't make it work, maybe that's because you weren't old enough to make it work. Maybe you weren't mature enough to do the work."

"I don't know," he said, staring down at his glass. "Maybe."

"That didn't sound very positive."

"No," he said, "it's not that. It's just there's been a lot of time under the bridge. You can never go backward."

"You don't have to," she said gently. "Life isn't about going backward. It's about making today happen the way you want it to, based on the new set of ground rules that you have for yourself."

"You have done a lot of thinking about this, haven't you?" he asked with a laugh.

Just then Diesel joined them. "Aren't you guys nice and cozy," he said. "What's all this heavy conversation? Wanna give me a clue? A little bit about it, not everything?"

She looked up and smiled and said, "We're discussing Jerricho's love life."

He looked at Jerricho, looked at her, and said, "Wow, now that's a great conversation." He added, "I didn't even know Jerricho had one."

"That's because his heart's still stuck with his ex-wife."

He looked over at Jerricho and said, "Really, man?"

Jerricho just smiled and said, "Eva's just taking it a little further than I would." He shrugged. "Basically my first love was my wife, but we've been divorced a long time now." He murmured, "At least twelve years."

"And is that something you want to go back to?"

"I wouldn't say that, but Eva's the one who keeps harping on it." And, at that, he said, "Here. Have a glass of wine, and let's eat."

Diesel said, "I'm starved."

Eva watched as Diesel took his place beside her. She sniffed the air and said, "Wow, is that what a clean male smells like?"

He burst out laughing. "Absolutely," he said. "Didn't

have a chance to shower earlier."

"Oh, I know," she said. "I'm the one who was tucked up against you all day."

He wrinkled his face. "Was it that bad?"

She laughed and shook her head. "No, I'm just kidding."

He said, "You're just a big tease."

"No," she said, "I'm just letting Jerricho off the hook from a conversation that he doesn't want to continue anymore."

At that, Jerricho looked at her and grinned. "You are very astute," he said. "And you've given me lots to think about."

"Good enough," she said. Then she turned to Diesel and said, "Now to you."

"TO ME FOR what?" Diesel asked. He lifted his glass, held it up to clink against hers, and said, "I thought we already decided that we would see each other when this was over."

At that, Jerricho laughed. "Wow," he said, "nice and fast."

"Well, yes, on both cases," she said. "I'm looking forward to getting back to normal."

"What is normal for you?" Jerricho asked curiously.

She smiled, shrugged, and said, "Not a whole lot. Work, home, work, home. The occasional visit with my father. Even fewer with my brother."

"That doesn't sound very awe-inspiring."

"Well, I made my work my life," she said quietly. "And I'm only just now realizing that, as I did that, I was losing out on other aspects of life," she added with a smile.

"Sometimes it takes something like this to shake us up, to give us a chance to reevaluate, and to see what we want to do differently."

"And that appears to be exactly what's happened," she said. "So we'll see what tomorrow brings."

"Good enough," Diesel said. They ate their way through a wonderful dinner, provided by their host, who none of them had nor would meet. One staff member took care of their needs. And, when dinner was over, Diesel looked over at her and said, "Needs to be bedtime."

"Already?" she said. She looked around at the massive yacht amid a softly churning ocean. "It's such a beautiful ship."

"It is, and we are guests, but we're not necessarily welcome to wander."

"Aha," she said. "So no sitting on the top deck to watch the sunset, right?"

He tilted his head to the side and said, "You know that I can ask, but we've been more or less requested to stay confined to our quarters."

"In that case," she said, "that's what we'll do."

As the staff member removed her plate, she looked up, smiled, and said, "Thank you. It was delicious." He inclined his head but didn't say a word.

Diesel watched him as he carted everything onto a trolley and pushed the trolley from the room. He already knew the drill, but she hadn't been in this situation before. Not that he had been exactly in one like this either though. He looked over at Jerricho. "Four-hour watches?"

"Yes," Jerricho said. "Can you take the first one?"

"Sure. I've had more sleep than you."

"I don't know about that," Jerricho said, "but I could

use some, being in the face of that wind all day. While piloting the ship is amazing, that wind just tuckers you out."

"I know," he said, as he looked over at Eva. "Come on. We'll go down to our quarters."

She stood, tossed back the last of her red wine, and said, "That should help me sleep."

"Good," Diesel said, "you need it too."

"Just seems like everything's a bit disjointed," she noted.

"And we're not done yet," he said.

"Too bad," she said. "But, if we're confined on this ship, and we can't move around, then maybe that's just for the best."

"They don't want anybody to be seen. They've done a big favor for us," he explained, "and we don't want to put them in any danger by somebody who might happen to be looking for us."

"I get it," she said, "believe me I do."

"Good," he said. "Come on then." And they went down a hallway and on to their quarters.

As they walked in, she sat down on the bed with a *thunk*. Diesel came in with her and sat down beside her. She looked at him in surprise. "Are you staying here with me?"

"One of us always will be," he said. "Jerricho's sleeping right now, so I'm here."

"Wow," she said, "I wasn't expecting that."

"We want to make sure that nothing else happens."

"I get that, but I thought we'd be safe here."

"You are," he said. "Stretch out and sleep."

"Right," she said, looking a little confused.

"We're only here for a little while," he said. "We're meeting up with somebody else. When we do, we'll be moving on."

"Right," she said, "so basically just roll over and crash. No nightclothes. No …?"

He immediately shook his head. "No, just in case we have to move fast."

"Well, that tells me where we're at relationship-wise, so fair warning right there," she said, with a sigh. But obediently she rolled over onto her side, pulled her pillow under her head, and asked, "Do you have an ETA for when we'll hit home?"

"Two to three days," he said.

"Still that long?"

"Remember. It's all about safety and security, not about speed."

"Got it," she said. She closed her eyes, and, just as she went under, Diesel spoke.

"By the way, how's that neck?"

"Nonexistent," she said, with a wave of her hand. "It's totally fine."

"Good," he said. "I'm sorry we had to do it."

"I'm not," she said, her eyes popping open. "I'm just grateful that you found it."

"Me too," he said. And, at that, he sat back and let her sleep. As soon as she was out, he pulled out his laptop and immediately signed into the Mavericks chat window and registered with Shane where they were and how far they had made it. **Jerricho's sleeping, and I'm on first watch.**

Shane immediately typed back, **Any danger?**

No.

Good. Get some sleep.

Can't. On watch.

You should be good for a bit, Shane came back.

Yeah, my nerves won't settle, he snapped. **I'll stay awake.**

Good, then work out the rest of your plan.

Already done, he wrote a trifle smugly.

At that, he signed off and researched a little more on her family and the company she worked for. It wasn't the company's full-time responsibility to keep her safe per se, but it did bring up some interesting questions about their manipulating media in order to keep investors involved. And, of course, anybody looking at hiring after something like this would keep a watch on the company. And still the kidnapping could have been completely random.

But now that they had found that tracker on Eva, Diesel was definitely a little worried. They had gotten free and clear, and the tracker couldn't possibly make it out to where they were, so he wasn't sure what was still bugging him. He also didn't know how long that tracker had been in there, and that was a concern too. But it was just one of many.

Unable to rest, he found articles on her father and read them avidly and about the lake he fished at and an interview. And then switched to her file on her mother and her brother and any other family members. But it was pretty scant information. Finally he closed his laptop, leaned his head back, and just dozed.

Every slightest movement had his eyes popping open to check to make sure all was well. But absolutely nothing was wrong, and, for that, he was grateful. By the time the four hours were up, he was ready to snooze. As he stood and opened the door, Jerricho walked toward him. "It's all clear," Diesel said.

"Good," Jerricho said. "Why don't you stay in there and sleep? I'll sit out here in one of the other rooms, with the door open, just to make sure we don't get any unexpected visitors."

Diesel nodded. "I can't see it happening," he said, "but …"

"But," Jerricho said, "we can't let down our guard, just in case."

With that, Diesel curled up beside Eva and fell asleep.

CHAPTER 13

EVA WOKE UP the next day to a repeat of the previous day. They went on another ship, met another ship, switched over, met another ship, switched over. And by the time she woke up two mornings later, she looked over at Diesel, who at this point was just sleeping beside her and holding her in his arms anytime they were alone. She smiled, reached up, stroked his cheek, and asked, "Did you get any sleep?"

Diesel just grunted.

She chuckled, got up, and said, "I'll have a shower."

"Do that," he said. "We land in an hour."

She stopped, turned, and looked at him. "Seriously?"

"Yes."

She gave a crow of delight and raced into the shower. By the time she was done, out, and dressed, she noticed that her clothes from the previous day were hung on the doorknob. "I didn't even question why you told me to strip down last night," she said. "I was so tired."

"I just wanted to make sure we got clean clothes," he said, sitting up, giving her a nice view of his chest. "I'll hop into the shower myself. Then we have breakfast and will see where the lay of the land is."

"Well, once I gave up worrying about it," she said, "I have to admit that this has been quite an adventure."

"And that's a good way to look at it too," he said, with a smile. "Just don't forget that, you know, theoretically danger is still all around us."

"And that's so hard to believe," she said. "I mean, it just seems so surreal."

"Maybe, but that doesn't change it though."

She nodded and watched as he walked into the bathroom, very naked, and smiled because he was just such a prime male. She deliberately turned her back as his heavily muscled cheeks walked past her. At the bathroom, he asked, "Are you okay?"

She snorted. "I'm fine," she said.

He looked at her with an odd glint in his eye.

She just laughed and said, "Go. Have your shower."

He shrugged and headed into the bathroom, and, when he came back out again, he had only a towel wrapped around him. She deliberately turned her gaze away and walked to stare out at the ocean. From what she saw, it was nothing but water and blue sky and just this faint line where the two met. "It's hard to believe just how vast the ocean is," she murmured.

"It is, indeed," he said. She heard him getting dressed behind her. And by the time the silence finally fell again, she sensed him coming closer. He wrapped his arms around her, pulled her back against him, kissed the top of her head, and said, "You okay?"

She nodded. "Absolutely," she said.

"You just seem different this morning."

She gave a smothered laugh, turned to look up at him, and, with a cheeky grin, said, "Let's just say that, if we were in any other scenario, when waking up to that beautiful male beside me, who then headed for the shower totally naked and got dressed behind me, I would not have allowed you to do so much without participation on my part."

His eyebrows shot up, and he grinned. "Well, that's good to know," he said.

"Ha!" she said. "You already knew."

"No, not really," he said. "I was deliberately not letting my mind roam in that direction."

"Right, because of where we're at," she said, with a heavy sigh.

"Yes," he admitted, "but it's just not the right thing to be focused on right now."

"I know, but I don't have the same discipline, and, when I woke up this morning …" she said, waggling her eyebrows.

He grinned, put a hand on either side of her face, tugged her closer, and gave her a kiss. "Later," he promised.

"Promises, promises," she said, with an airy wave of her hand.

He burst out laughing and said, "Come on. It's time to go."

"Breakfast?"

"We're having a light breakfast, and then we should see the harbor." With that, she raced to the door. He shook his head and said, "Let's make sure that you're ready and packed up to go."

As she looked around, she realized how little she had with her. There was nothing to pack up. They only had one bag between them.

And then he held out his hand and said, "Let's go." As they walked out, he said, "We're eating on deck today."

"You mean, I'll actually get to be outside for once?" she asked. "It's been really hard being on these beautiful yachts and not allowed to go outside."

"The whole idea of keeping you hidden is to keep you hidden," he murmured.

"I got it," she said. "Doesn't mean that it wasn't a terrible shame, and I didn't want to get back outside and enjoy the experience."

"You ever been on one of these before?"

"No," she cried out, "and that's why it's such a shame. So many experiences right now that I would love to really enjoy, but because I'm hiding away..." And she just shrugged and said, "But it is what it is, and hopefully it'll be over soon."

"That's the attitude," he said. He reached out, snagged her arm, and said, "Come on. Let's go." And they raced up the stairs.

As she came out on the deck, she stopped and gasped because the harbor was right up ahead of them. "Land!"

"It is," he said, "but we're still probably a good forty minutes out."

He motioned at the table, where Jerricho sat. He smiled at them and said, "Don't you two look refreshed."

"I feel much better," she said, "and just even sitting outside is huge."

He nodded. "It's so hard to stay inside when the world around you is looking so much more promising and inviting."

"Exactly," she said. "And I really do get why. It's just sad that I don't have a chance to spend some time here and to enjoy it and to be a tourist for a change."

"You can always come back," he said.

"I probably couldn't even begin to afford a holiday like this," she said, with a laugh. "These are superyachts."

"They are, and very few of them are commissioned for

the type of work that we needed them to do," he said. "It's patriots all the way, and we appreciate their assistance in this matter."

"Absolutely," she said, "and, for that reason alone, I understand not overstaying our welcome."

"Well, the family is actually on board right now," he said, "and they are on the far side, keeping to themselves, but the yacht is actually big enough that we don't have to cross each other."

"Well, it's much appreciated," she said warmly. Just then their breakfast was served, and she laughed to see eggs and sausage and pancakes. "This makes me think I won't eat again for a while," she said, with a sidelong look at him.

"And we might not," he said, "so eat while there's food."

Nobody needed to tell her twice. She tucked in until she was full. She pushed back her plate and said, "Wow, that was really good. Not only is it a gorgeous place and a gorgeous view, but the food is excellent too."

"Glad you enjoyed it," he murmured. "And as you can see, we're coming up to the docks."

She looked and got up and walked to the railing, as the beautiful yacht came up against what could have been a private pier. "So we just walk off?"

"Did you have a better idea?"

"No, but we've gone from one clandestine method to another," she said. "I just can't imagine that I get to go free and clear now."

"And you'd be right," Diesel said, with a chuckle.

She sighed. "Where are we going next then?"

"Into that car up there." He pointed to a black car that pulled up at the top of the wharf. With the three of them together, they headed toward the vehicle.

"Do you keep track of whether anybody is watching us? Or do we still think that any danger's associated with me?"

"No way to know," he said, "so we're not taking any chances, until we get you home."

"And yet that in itself is an oxymoron because that's where I was taken from," she murmured.

"I know," he said, "but we will figure it out."

"Right."

At that, he walked up the last few ramp-like inclines and opened the back seat to help her in. The driver popped the trunk, and Diesel put their bags in the back, and then he hopped in beside her. Jerricho hopped into the front passenger seat. And just like that, they drove away.

She studied the man whose face she saw in the mirror but only part of it. She'd never seen him before. The driver didn't look at her directly. He was dressed in a black suit, and she had absolutely no idea who he was. She sighed, as she looked over at Diesel. "Now where?"

"We're flying out tonight," he said calmly.

"Good," she said in delight. "Hopefully home?"

"Yep," he said, "and I know it's been quite the trip so far, but I thank you for your patience."

She sighed. "It sounds incredibly immature of me to even complain," she said. "I mean, let's be obvious. You've done a lot to … everything you've done has been to keep me safe, so I'm just glad we're finally going home."

And, at that, they were driven to a small hotel, and, when they went inside, she thought they'd be in another hotel room. Instead it looked more like a boardroom. She looked around in surprise. "So …"

And Diesel just laughed and said, "We're here until our flights."

"Okay," she said. "In that case, what will we do here?"

"We'll do nothing," he said.

She groaned, buried her head in her hands, and said, "I'm so tired of doing nothing."

"What would you like to do?"

She perked up. "Shop?"

"Nope," he said.

She groaned. "How about … be a tourist and go sight-seeing?"

"No," he said.

She groaned. "Read a book? Watch TV?"

"Absolutely. Anything inside that doesn't require leaving."

She sighed. "Fine then." And she headed to the TV and she turned it on.

"EVA'S HANDLING IT pretty well," Jerricho said beside him.

Diesel looked up, saw Eva sitting before the TV on the far side, and nodded. "Like anybody in her position, she just wants it over with."

"And, of course, this is hardly a romantic way to spend time together."

At that, Diesel rolled his eyes. "Quit harping on the romance," he said. "This is all about real life."

"Romance is real life too," she called out over the TV.

He groaned. "You aren't part of this conversation."

"Maybe I should be," she said, looking back and flashing him that bright grin that he was starting to really enjoy.

"Not really," he said.

She shrugged. "You can't hold all the conversations

yourself, you know?" she said. "That's just being greedy."

"What more do you want to talk about, then?" he asked in surprise.

"Nothing," she said. "I just …" And then she stopped and said, "Well, I just really want to go home."

"Got it," he said. "We'll get you there soon enough." He added, "And I know it doesn't feel like we're doing anything fast because we're deliberately not trying to do the speedy route, but I want to make sure that you get home safe."

"Got it." She kicked her feet up, turned her attention back to the television.

He looked over at Jerricho. "Any concerns?"

"No," he said slowly, "but still something's just niggling in the back of my mind."

"Me too," Diesel said. "I just don't know how or why. I think we'll be fine to head out of here and to go to Wisconsin. We got several flights to make that trip. But she's right. She wasn't kidnapped from the lab. Yet the lab was using their marketing efforts to build up the lab's visibility to bring in investment money."

"It's quite possible that they overstated their findings," Jerricho said.

"Well, we've certainly seen stock manipulation happen time and time again," he said. "This wouldn't be any different."

"No. Do you think they had anything to do with it?"

"I hope not, for her sake," Diesel said slowly. "It has crossed my mind, but I haven't been able to find anything."

"Me either," he said. "And, if they did, then what?" Jerricho asked.

"Then she's not safe even back at work," he said, his tone low so she couldn't hear him. "And that in itself is even more upsetting because, after all this, you'd like to think that we're taking her back to where she's safe and sound, but is she?" Diesel looked over at Eva and called out, "What would your boss be doing right now?"

"My boss?" Eva said. "He'd be in his office, probably talking to investors, talking to the shareholders, fielding questions from the other techs. Why?"

"I don't know. I just wonder if he had anything to do with this."

"I don't think so. He's a people guy. I don't think he's somebody who thinks that far ahead of what could happen if somebody stole his scientist. Did he ask for donations because of my research contributions? I guess it's possible. Or maybe the shareholders donated money? I don't know." She turned to face them better, and she said, "Since this started, I wondered because I do know that I've seen them exaggerate some of our findings to get more public interest, and that's frowned upon in the scientific world. So I don't really know what's going on there. I just can't imagine that he thought that this would really be a good answer. Generally I would have said he was somebody with heart."

"Nationality?"

"American," she said. Then she frowned. "But his wife's Chinese."

"His wife is Chinese?"

She nodded. "And she's a scientist too."

"And where does she work?"

"She's on the board of directors," she said. "She doesn't come into the lab anymore."

"Any idea if she had anything to do with this?"

"But I don't know why she would."

"Right," he said, staring out in the distance. "I just feel

like something else is involved."

"I'm sure there is," she said with a nod. "How will we ever find out what that is? And to find it out before I go back to work? And, of course, we could be looking at it completely wrong. And accusing people having absolutely nothing to do with this."

"And that's always the challenge, isn't it?" Jerricho said. He looked at Diesel. "I'll pick up on the research."

He nodded. "I will too."

Both of them grabbed their laptops. Both jumped into the Mavericks chat window and asked for information about the company, her boss, and the boss's wife, looking for connections, looking for any thread that would lead back to the lab in China. Immediately Diesel was sent links to portfolios and articles that he sat and devoured. An amazing amount of information about the company and about the boss was here. But very little about the wife.

Until he caught one little line which said that she had been born and raised in mainland China and came over only after meeting the boss at a conference. He highlighted that and sent it both to Jerricho, who was sitting beside him, and to Shane on the other end of the chat.

Jerricho looked at it, one eyebrow raised. "Are you thinking this might be it?"

"It's hard to say," he said, "but what if she's a mole? What if she came to recruit what the lab in China needs? In China, what she did was work in the lab all the time. And yet, since coming to the US, she hasn't."

He looked over at Eva to find her engrossed in her TV show. He hesitated to ask her and to raise more suspicions, but just then Jerricho pulled up an article and turned his laptop so Diesel saw it.

He quickly picked up the laptop from him and read it, and nodded. "That's interesting too."

Because right there, in black-and-white, was the woman's brother. He worked at the same Boston lab as Eva did. Diesel frowned at that, wondering if that made any difference. Was it wrong? Or was it just a typical family affair? He knew many families hired within to keep the business flowing that way. It's hardly illegal, and normally it certainly wasn't even suspicious. As his laptop buzzed, he looked down and said, "Believe it or not, it's time to go."

She smiled and said, "Yay!" And she hopped up, walked to the door, and said, "Come on. Come on. Let's go. Our future's waiting."

"Our future is always waiting," Diesel said as he got up. "The fact of the matter is, we have to make sure that the right one is waiting for us."

She waited impatiently, as he packed up his gear, and soon enough they were all heading down to the car, taking them to the airport. The whole way he kept checking in on a Spidey instinct to see if anything was setting off alarms. And there wasn't, but it didn't stop that one nagging suspicion from being a bit of an irritant. As they got to the airport and had to wait before going through clearance, he checked with Shane on the Russian agents' progress.

Both of the Russians we had tagged via facial recognition leaving the Chinese lab have been scanned returning to Russia.

Anyone with them?

No. They came home without their operative after we informed them of his death prior to their arrival.

Good. Any idea what the airport shutdown was all about back in Manila?

We're hoping it's because of the Russians, but we

don't know. They didn't go through the main airport, so their method out of the country is unknown.

Well, like us, I'm sure they had another way out entirely.

CHAPTER 14

WHEN THE TRIO finally landed on US soil, Eva stopped for a moment, inhaled the smog-filled air outside New York, before he whisked her away to another airport and another flight. "Why couldn't we have stayed there?"

"Again, decoy," he said. "I always try to keep people hopping."

"Wow," she said, "you're really going to great lengths to keep me hidden."

"Absolutely," he said with a smile. "I don't want anything to happen to you."

There was just that note in his voice that made her believe him. "Aww, that's so sweet," she murmured.

"Hardly," he said.

"You just don't want all the time that you invested in keeping me safe to go to waste," she said, with a chuckle. He squeezed her fingers. She looked at him in surprise. "Hey, I was just teasing," she added gently.

He nodded. "Of course you are," he said, "but I would not be happy to lose you."

And, at that, she smiled and said, "Got it."

If she thought that the trip was almost over, they weren't done for another seven hours. When they finally came into the airport at the outskirts of Wisconsin, she stood in disbelief. Because there, in front of her, was her father. She cried out, "Oh, my God," and she raced forward into his arms. He held her tight, and she felt the tears just pouring down her cheeks.

"They didn't tell me," she babbled. "They didn't tell me." Her father hugged her close, just rocking her gently, until she calmed down. Finally she pulled back and looked up to see tears in his eyes, and she wiped the tears in her own. "Oh, my God," she said, "he didn't tell me."

Her father smiled and said, "And he didn't need to either. It was supposed to be a surprise."

"See? I've been traveling for days," she cried out, feeling the exhaustion in her own voice.

"I know," he said, gently pushing the hair off her face, leaning forward to kiss her on the cheek. "I'm so glad you made it," he whispered.

"It's been so rough," she said. "And yet, at the same time"—she smiled and looked back at Diesel and Jerricho, who just stood there, allowing the two to have a moment alone—"it's been really good."

"I hear that."

She looked at him in surprise and said, "Did you talk to him?"

"I've have spoken to Diesel a couple times."

She spun and stared accusingly at Diesel. "All this time and you didn't tell me!"

"I thought it might be a nice surprise," Diesel said in a mild tone.

She glared at him and then realized that he would do what he thought he should do, and it didn't really matter. Neither did it really matter in this instance. She turned back and hugged her father hard. "We were coming to you, you know?"

"I know," he said. "And rather than surprising me, I decided to surprise you."

She smiled, hugged him again, and turned to look back at Diesel with a glaring look.

And he just smiled and said, "You're welcome."

She thought about it, burst out laughing, walked over, and gave Diesel a big hug. "Thank you so much," she whispered. "It's so good to see him."

"Well, we were coming to see him anyway," he murmured, "so …" And then he stepped forward and shook her father's hand. "Nice to finally meet you, Greg."

"Likewise," Greg said, eyeing Diesel up and down. He looked over his daughter. "Well, I can see why you waited this long."

She looked at him in confusion.

"To find the right man," he said. "This is obviously the right man."

She flushed bright red. "Maybe," she said, "that remains to be seen."

He laughed, whispered in Eva's ear, "That man there took care of your brother, put him in rehab, so he gets points in my book."

She was stunned into silence, looking from her dad to Diesel.

"Come on then," Greg said. "I've got my truck." With that, everybody piled into his vehicle, and he drove them back to the cabin on the lake. As she stared out the window, all the images brought back memories, and she smiled. "I forgot … how peaceful it is," she said.

"Take the men down to the lake," he said, "then you'll really see some peacefulness." As they drove, she pointed out landmarks to the two men.

"How often do you come here?" Jerricho asked her.

"Not enough," she said, as she feasted her eyes on the small town, as they drove through it. They drove for another couple miles to a turnoff, and she said, "I forgot how much I loved it here."

"She used to come here when her mother was still alive," her father said, "when she was just a kid. Her roots are here."

"Interesting," he said. "Why didn't you come back and live here?"

"Well, I had to make a living," she said with a laugh.

"Do you still though?"

"I don't know. It's one of the things that I have to reassess, isn't it?"

"If you want to stay," her dad said, "you know you're welcome."

"And that would be a welcomed respite from the mess that I've just come out of," she said.

"I'm perfectly capable of keeping you safe," Greg said.

"Well, I don't know about that in this instance." As soon as they got to the cabin, she hopped out and said to her dad, "I'll walk down to the lake."

"Take Diesel with you. I hear he likes to fish."

"I do," Diesel said, "but I'm not the fisherman you are."

Greg looked over at Jerricho. "Do you fish?"

Jerricho admitted, "I've never had a chance to try." Her father stopped in shock and stared at him. Jerricho gave him a wide grin. "But I'm happy to try now."

"Damn right you are," Greg said. "First lesson is, we have to clean a bunch." He explained further, "I was out this morning, so we'll have grilled trout for dinner."

She laughed at that. "And you'll have it for breakfast,

and you'll have it for dinner again too," she said. And she headed down toward the lake. She knew Diesel would be behind her, even if she hadn't necessarily invited him. And, sure enough, as she got to the dock, he came up right behind her.

"Are you trying to get away?" he asked curiously.

"Nope," she said, "but I had to trust that you were behind me the whole way."

He smiled and nodded. "And you're right." He looked at the lake and smiled. "Now this is beautiful."

"I know," she said. "We've had this property … I think it's been in the family for generations."

"And it's worth hanging on to," he said. "It's lovely."

"It's a great place to come and visit," she said. "I'm not sure I'm necessarily ready to live here though."

"I get it." He nodded. "You could also be closer though."

"Again, that's all in that possibility of *what do I want to do with my life now*," she said. She held his hand and said, "Let's walk down to the end of the pier. It's my favorite place."

And as they walked to the end of the dock and stepped down one more level, so they were on the dock that floated on the water, they made their way to the very end. She loved listening to the birds and to the water lap up against the shore.

"This," she said, "is stunning." She stood here, watching as the sun slowly sank on the hillside across from them. "And I didn't think I'd actually get here."

He closed his arms around her, held her tight, and said, "I promised."

"You did at that," she said, "and thank you. I'm so grateful to be home."

They stood here in a moment of quiet contemplation. She turned in his arms, looked up at him, and kissed him gently. "And that's not out of gratitude. Then she stopped and said, "Okay, so that one's out of gratitude." Then she flung her arms around his neck and kissed him long and hard. When she finally broke free, she said, "That one wasn't." She smiled when she realized his breathing was unsteady and his gaze had gone dark.

He pulled her back into his arms. "Well, that's a damn good thing," he said, "because this is a little bit too passionate for gratitude."

"Hey, whatever works," she said, chuckling.

He pulled her back into his arms and kissed her long and deep, until she was a wet noodle clinging to him. "That," she said, "was lovely."

"Yeah, well, you're staying at your dad's place now," he said. "It's hardly private time for us."

"Actually," she said, "we'll be staying in another cabin all on our own. Dad has the main cabin, but I always stay in a little cabin off to the side." She turned and pointed.

He looked at it, smiled, and said, "Now that is an idea I can get behind." She laughed, and, with a last look at the lake, they headed back up to the main cabin.

DIESEL LOOKED AROUND. His heart loved the scene, but the guard in him said it was too open, and yet there were too many places for somebody else to hide. And, as he studied the cabin off to the side, he realized it was perfectly private, which would be absolutely wonderful for them for the night, but it would also be a place where he didn't want her on her own. They could have a predator in there in no time, and she wouldn't have a chance to fight or to argue. And nobody would know of the attack, if her father were out fishing all day on the lake.

As they walked into the kitchen, Jerricho looked up with a big grin and said, "Hey, my first fish." He pointed to the cutting board.

"Good," Diesel said.

"Tomorrow you can try catching your first ones," her father said. "Up at the crack of dawn. Hope you're an early riser."

Jerricho looked at Diesel and asked, "You or me first in the morning?"

"You go," Diesel said.

Jerricho, with a knowing look, said, "That works." He added, "Apparently I'm sleeping in the main cabin."

"Right," Diesel said. "Then Greg can wake you up that early."

"Works for me," he said. "I'm looking forward to it."

"Good. That's the way it's supposed to be."

Dinner was a lighthearted affair.

Diesel's heart was gently delighted to see the relationship between father and daughter. A lot of affection, lots of little touches, hugs, as they went around each other. Both happy that each other was safe and content to be here. By the time dinner was over, she was yawning. He shook his head. "Time for bed again."

She grinned at him. "You've been telling me that for days," she protested.

"And every time I turn around, you're falling asleep over your food," he warned.

Her father nodded. "She's always been like that. She'll go, go, go, and then, all of a sudden, she'll drop."

"I am not that bad," she said.

"Yes, you absolutely are," Jerricho said, "but because I'm getting up at five in the morning, I won't stay up late myself either." And stepping outside, the two men sorted out their four-hour watches. "What do you think? Do we need to stand on watch?"

"It's really hard to know, isn't it?" Diesel said. "We're home. She should be safe. It should be over with. But it doesn't feel that way."

Jerricho nodded. "No," he said, "my gut says it's bad news."

"Mine too," he said. "If you want to take first watch, I'll stand second."

"The trouble is," Jerricho said, "I'll be awake, and you won't be sleeping."

And, with that, Diesel laughed and headed back inside. Diesel looked over at Eva, who was falling asleep on the chair. He walked over, bent down, and scooped her up in his arms. She protested but was mumbling. He shook his head, looked over at her father, and said, "Is there plumbing in that little cabin?"

He nodded. "There is actually. We put it in just before my wife passed away."

"Good," he said. "I might as well get her there, while I can still see the pathway." And, with that, he headed out the door, Jerricho with him, carrying their bags. As they got to the other cabin, Jerricho stepped in first, did a quick search, came back, and said, "You'll be fine here."

Diesel carried her in and laid her on the bed, and she just rolled over, pulled the pillow under her head, and crashed.

"She always like that?" Jerricho asked.

"Apparently," Diesel said. "Every time we tell her it's naptime, she just crashes."

"Must be nice," he said.

"Yeah, I hear you." At that, they turned and headed back out again.

"I'll send you a message at two a.m.," he said.

"Sounds good." Diesel walked back inside the cabin, tired despite himself. It was only ten p.m., but, if he could sleep now, that would be the best. He quickly used the facilities, brushed his teeth, gave his face a good scrub down, and then headed into the bedroom. As he looked at Eva, he realized she hadn't even shifted. She was sound asleep, fully dressed. Well, that would not end up well.

He took off her shoes and socks, rolled her onto her back, divested her of her jeans, and then half-sitting her up, with her mumbling and protesting the whole way, he managed to get the T-shirt off her. He would have left the T-shirt on, if he could get the bra off, but, as it was, it was that much harder to get any cooperation out of her. Finally he just picked her up, tucked her under the blankets, then quickly divested himself of his clothes and crawled in beside her.

As he lay here on the bed, his arms under his head, he thought about everything they've gone through and how far and how slow they had traveled, and he realized that there was absolutely no reason for anybody to be following them, but he still couldn't shake that weird feeling. He rolled over, pulled her up against him, and closed his eyes. He slept solid and deep until he heard that whistle.

As soon as he heard it, his eyes opened. He checked his watch and confirmed it was two o'clock. He slipped out from under the covers, pulled on his boxers, jeans and a T-shirt and walked out to the deck. There he raised a hand, as he saw Jerricho standing on the porch of the main cabin. Jerricho walked inside and headed to bed. He would be lucky if he got three hours now, after what Greg had said about getting up at five. Maybe Greg would take it a little easier on Jerricho, but Diesel doubted it.

He stood here for a long moment, enjoying the fresh crisp air on the lake. So much cooler here, being at a cabin in the summer. It would heat up during the day but then would cool down beautifully in the evening. Right now it was clear and refreshing. He sat here on the stoop for the longest time, thoroughly loving the opportunity to be here. At a sound, he walked back inside the cabin to see her sitting up, pushing her tangled hair from her eyes.

She stared at him. "What time is it?" she croaked out.

"It's three-thirty," he said. "Go back to sleep." She lay back on the bed and stared up at the ceiling and groaned. "I hate waking up at this hour."

"Why is that?" he asked.

"Because it's so hard to get back to sleep."

"It'll be fine," he murmured.

She smiled and then winced. "How come I'm still wearing my bra?"

"Because I didn't want to strip you right down to the skin," he said.

She sighed, got up, and walked to the bathroom, and, when she came back out, she had on a nightie. She said, "I always leave some clothes here." And, with that, she yawned and crawled back into bed.

He walked around the cabin. Every time he checked on her, she was in a different position.

Finally she groaned, sat up, and announced, "I can't sleep."

"You want to sit outside here with me?" he asked.

She thought about it and nodded. "Sure." And sat beside him. "I always loved it out here in the evening," she said.

"I don't think three-thirty, almost four a.m. now, is *evening,*" he said, with a chuckle.

She smiled and nodded. "It's also cool." He patted his lap, and she crawled onto his lap and curled up. "I forgot how warm you were," she said, snuggling in close.

"Well, you're not wearing much this time," he said.

"So, if you're on watch," she said, "I guess no hanky-panky, huh?"

A rumble moved up his chest as he chuckled. "Shouldn't, no," he said.

"*Shouldn't* but that doesn't mean *no,*" she said. She looked up at him and said, "What better way to keep an eye on me? I mean, other than keeping two hands on me."

AND, AT THAT, Eva slipped her hands underneath Diesel's T-shirt and up across his belly and chest. He sucked in his breath and said, "Just because we think we're safe ..."

"I know," she said. "I so desperately want to believe we're safe."

"I know," he said. And she started to kiss him on the side of the neck up to his ear, blowing gently inside, and he felt his belly tighten and his groin swell. "That's definitely dangerous."

"Nope," she said, "I'll take this as a nightcap. To help me get back to sleep again."

"Sex is a way to go back to sleep?"

"God, I hope so," she said. "I'm so tired, and I'm so wound up that I don't even know what I'm worried about."

"Are you worried?"

"I am," she said. "It just feels like it's not over."

He didn't say anything.

She looked at him. "Why can't we grab a few minutes just for ourselves?"

"I didn't say we can't," he said. He gave himself thirty seconds to think about it, and then he stood up with her in his arms. And, making her laugh, he carried her all the way back to the bedroom, where he tossed her gently on the bed. She immediately popped up onto her knees and pulled her nightie up over her head and tossed it onto the bed beside her. He stared, his breath frozen, desperately trying to escape his chest. "My God," he murmured, "you're just gorgeous."

She was lean, trim, full-breasted, and gorgeous. He gave a happy sigh, as he quickly pulled off his T-shirt over his head and chucked off his jeans and boxers. He stepped forward, and she stared at him in surprise.

"Talk about gorgeous," she murmured, her hands reaching eagerly for his erection. He tried to step back, but she had already caught him, her hands avid as they explored his hips, then his testicles and his groin. When they slipped down his thighs to come back up between his thighs, he shuddered and laid her back down on the bed. "It'll be well over," he said. "You can't do that to me."

"Well, I can," she said, wrapping a thigh around him and rubbing her pelvis against him. "Because I want this as much as you do. At the same time, it feels like we've been heading for this stage for a long time."

"We've hardly known each other but several days," he protested.

"I know," she said, "but what we do know, we like each other."

"No arguments there," he said, his voice thick. He kissed her rather desperately. But, when she wrapped her thighs around his hips and started to rub at a faster and faster pace, he groaned and pushed his weight down against her. "Slow down," he whispered. "Slow down."

She smiled, looked up, kissed him gently, and said, "Nope, not going to."

CHAPTER 15

NO WAY IN hell would Eva slow down. She felt the passion riding her hard and fast. She flipped him over onto his back, and, before he had a chance to react, she lowered herself onto his shaft and ground her hips tight against his. She gasped and cried out, arching her back, as the first of the shock waves shuddered through her. He reached up, held her hips tight, and ground up higher against her, sending even more shock waves through her.

While she still shuddered, he slowly explored the heart of her, open and waiting, spreading the moisture around, gently teasing the tiny nub before his hand slid up over her belly to cup and explore her breasts. When he finally couldn't stand it, he sat up and pulled her toward him, so he could awkwardly suckle her breasts, first one and then the other, showering each nipple with his attention.

Feeling his way, he explored and stroked that space between her buttocks and upper spine and over her shoulders and down and around her arms. When he finally lay beneath her, shuddering again, his hips moving, driving up slowly and slowly, she leaned over and grabbed his shoulders and whispered, "Ready for round two?"

"You might be," he said, "but I'm desperate for round one." And he lunged upward. She took over the rhythm and started to ride, slow, deep, then long and fast. And, when he exploded beneath her, she collapsed on top of him, feeling the shock waves once again rippling through her. She lay atop him, covered in sweat, enjoying the peace and the release of the tension. "That," he said, "was beautiful."

"It was," she said. She yawned and said, "Now you know something? I might go to sleep."

He snorted. "That's fine," he said. "You get to. I don't."

She laughed. "You're right." And then rolled over.

DIESEL PULLED THE blankets up over her, kissed her tenderly on the temple, and said, "Just sleep." He got up, put on his boxers and jeans, and stepped out into the living room. They'd left the front door open. As he stepped out onto the deck and took several deep breaths, something cold and hard and round and metal was shoved against his spine.

He didn't move for the longest moment. And then slowly, he turned. With his hands in the air, he faced somebody he'd never seen before. "Interesting," he said. "Hired gun or somebody who'll do the job himself?"

"I'll do the job myself," said the guy in front of him.

"And do I get to know who you are?"

"I'm her boss. "Everybody started to make inquiries into my wife's position in the country and in the company and then her ties to China," he said. "Of course they look at that. They always see me as a dupe. I'm nobody's dupe."

And, at that, Diesel nodded. "Of course not," he said, "but she was a really good cover, wasn't she?"

"She was. I was born in China. We knew each other when we were children and always planned to get married," he said. "We set this up a long time ago. And because she's not involved, nobody can blame her for anything or tie her to anything."

"It still doesn't make any sense," he said.

"Nope, but we've had a high turnover. I'm sure Eva told you that," he said. "And mostly because I was singling out the decent scientists, hoping that we could find the proper cures over in China. But we never could. Eva was the next on the list to be tried."

"I didn't realize Paul and Marge both worked for you."

"They did. She didn't tell you that? Not the same location though."

"No, not so clearly," he said, frowning. "But then I didn't actually ask." He shook his head. "What a fool."

"Yeah, you see? A bright young man, like you, can get completely sidetracked by a woman." He said, "That's why my wife does her job so well. She sidetracks everybody into thinking something completely different, and then, when they start looking at her connections, and they get suspicious, they can't find anything. So it all eases away again."

"Whereas you're in it together," he said.

"Yep, our company's failing. I have to keep pulling these tricks to get more investors. We're about to shut it all down, go bankrupt actually," he said, "and that's a good thing."

"And why is that?"

"Because, once we're bankrupt, nobody will take too much notice," he said. "We'll go back to China, and I'm not exactly sure what we'll do from there," he admitted. "I know some of the company men over there aren't very happy with us. Because of what happened. But it's not our fault that Eva escaped. Matter of fact, we'll blame that on you."

"And you'd be right," Diesel said mildly. "You would be very right. But that doesn't stop here or now. Why come here and take her out?"

"Well, we can't have any threads left, can we? And then everybody involved in that lab is truly gone," he said. "That's just the way of the world."

"So why are you not gone?"

"Well, because I am one of the bosses," he said.

Diesel smiled and shook his head. "No." He said, "You were one of the bosses as long as you were delivering. You're no longer delivering, and you've caused a problem, so you know you're about to be eliminated yourself."

"Well, if anybody else worked for us, then that would be the truth, but I'm definitely the boss," he said, "and I call the shots."

"I'm surprised you're here, doing the work yourself."

"I would let my brother-in-law do it because he really wanted to, but I figured that, if anybody saw another Asian moving around the countryside, that would be too memorable."

"Yes, it would," he said. "So what's the plan here?"

"That's easy. It'll be a murder-suicide. I'll shoot her, set you up for it, and then you'll shoot yourself."

"Wow, and why would I want to do that?"

"The oldest reasons in the book," he said. "You fell in love. She was just using you, and you couldn't take it. In a fit of anger, you killed her. Once you realized what you had done, you couldn't live with yourself, and you killed yourself."

Diesel stared at him in surprise. "That cut-and-dried, huh?"

"Life really is cut-and-dried," he said. "Those with power use it. Those without want it and try everything they can do to get it. And we spend all our time making sure we hang on to it."

"Got it," he said. "Where's your wife now?"

"She's in town, waiting for me," he said. "We've already shut down everything. My brother-in-law's doing the last of it now."

"And all because Eva escaped?"

"Of course. If we'd managed to take her out over there, then we wouldn't have this problem. Yet you managed to get her back here again, so I'll blame you for all this."

"Right," he said, "sorry to hear that." He nodded toward the doorway. "And of course you have to take me out before you go after her."

"Of course," he said.

At that, another voice entered the fray. "Isn't that just too bad then," Eva said, leaning against the doorway.

Her boss turned to look at her and immediately backed up, so his gun could cover both of them.

She didn't even appear concerned. She leaned against the door, her arms crossed over her nightie. "You know what? I kept considering why you would do this, and I just didn't have any idea. But I knew something was wrong. I knew a connection was here that I just couldn't put two and two together."

"Well, that's why I'm the boss, and you're not," he said.

"Really?" she said, with a smile. "I don't think so."

He looked at her, confused. "Why are you not worried?" he asked.

"What's to be worried about?" she said. "I trust Diesel."

Diesel looked at her, seeing the relaxed, almost too relaxed, attitude in her stance and heard the ever-so-slight owl call behind him. "You know something?" he said, looking over at her boss. "I don't even remember what your name is.

But, considering that your wife is close by, are there any last words you wanted to say to her?"

"What are you talking about?" he said irritably. "I'm not going anywhere."

"Oh, you are," he said. "You just don't know it yet."

"That's BS. I'm the one with the gun." He motioned at him. "Get back into the cabin right now."

"And if I say no?"

The gunman lifted his gun and said, "I will shoot you right now," he said. "Enough of this. Go back inside."

Diesel looked over at Eva, smiled, and said, "Three, two, one." And she dashed back inside, and he dropped to the deck.

A single shot fired out, and, as Diesel watched, the gunman stopped and stared, even as a red circle appeared in his forehead, and then he crumpled to the ground. The boss didn't even fire his gun, his finger never even clenched the trigger. It was all over in half a second.

Diesel bounced to his feet and kicked the handgun away. He immediately called out to Jerricho, "The wife is the other half of the team, and she's probably at the driveway."

Jerricho disappeared.

Diesel raced inside and asked Eva, "Are you okay?"

"I'm fine," Eva said, shivering. "I contacted Jerricho."

"Perfect," he said. "You did right."

"Oh, my God," she said. "If I had gone back to work …"

"They would have taken you out, yes. We'll get the whole story as we investigate further," he said, "but the wife's brother's also involved. He's been doing this for a while. You didn't tell me that Paul used to work with you."

"Well, yes, he did a long time ago."

"You have any idea how long Paul worked for your boss? Both Paul and Marge worked for the same company."

"Oh, my God," she said. "Marge, too?"

"Marge used to work at your company too," he said. "The boss has been sorting through his employees and choosing who would go to the Chinese lab."

"And it was all for what?"

"Money," he said. "They didn't have enough money to keep this company going. He figured China would be better, and, if he didn't have to pay any wages, it would be better yet again."

She stared at him in shock. "Kidnapped just … just to save him money, save him business expenses?" she said, hopelessness in her voice.

He opened his arms, and she raced into them. "Yes," he said, "just for money."

She burst into tears, and he held her close. "I had such high hopes," she said, "when I went into this industry."

"And there's no reason," he said, "that you have to give up on that either."

She nodded, and he saw that it would take a toll on her. She looked up at the main cabin and said, "Do you think my father's okay?"

"I'm sure he's fine," he said, "but we can go check on him."

She smiled, nodded, and said, "We need to make sure that we catch the other half of that lovely relationship," she said.

They heard another owl call at that time, cutting through the silence, and Diesel said, "And that's Jerricho saying that he's got her."

Eva raced inside, pulled on some clothes, and, as she

reached out and grabbed his hand. "It's too unbelievable. After everything we've done, everything we've been through," she said, "to even think that this was possible?"

"I know," he said, "and I'm sorry."

"It's not your fault," she said. "It's … None of it's your fault."

"Well, it isn't, but it is," he said, "and the end result is, it's all good now."

"As long as my father's okay," she said. And, as they walked up, Jerricho held on to the woman being forced to come toward them. Her gaze was wide, huge, and she wore a tight gag, and her hands were tied up behind her. Jerricho looked over at Diesel and said, "I've put a call out for a pickup."

"Good," he said. "I'll go check on Greg." He walked into the cabin, found Greg sound asleep, but, as it was almost five o'clock, chances were he wouldn't stay asleep for long. Diesel returned to join Jerricho and said, "Let's take them up to the road and have the pickup there. Let's keep the ugliness out of here, as much as we can."

Eva looked at him, smiled, and said, "Thank you for that."

"You got it." With Jerricho's help, Diesel picked up the dead gunman, and Jerricho picked up his wife, and they carried the two of them to a small pullout. With the woman and her dead husband, they waited. It wasn't long before a vehicle arrived. Both, the dead husband and living wife, were collected. One team went down to the smaller cabin and did a quick sweep, cleaning out anything as needed, and then they were gone.

As Diesel walked back into the main cabin, Jerricho at his side, Greg sat with a pot of coffee on the back deck.

Greg looked up, smiled, and said, "You know when you said you were early birds, I didn't think you meant it," he said. "But if you're raring to go fishing this badly ..." And he wrung his hands together with joy.

Jerricho chuckled. "I could do with some fishing out in that lake," he said. "Something to remind me about Mother Earth and all the good things in life."

"You got it," Greg said. As he walked past his daughter, he reached down and gave her a big hug and said, "You do know how to bring home good men." And, with that, he disappeared.

Diesel walked over, picked her up, held her close, and said, "It's over."

She looked up, smiled, and said, "Thank you."

"You're welcome," he said. "It's been a tough go, but it's over."

She sighed, wrapped her arms around him, and the two of them watched as Jerricho and her father gently wrangled together as they headed down to the lake. "Does Jerricho really want to go fishing?"

"You know what? I think he actually does."

"Oh, thank heavens," she said. "I *really* don't like fishing."

He burst out laughing and said, "Well, have you got something better you want to do today?"

She looked up, gave him a cheeky grin, and said, "Absolutely. I'm pretty sure we didn't finish what we started earlier."

He gave a shout of laughter and said, "Well, in that case, I think we need to spend a little bit of time together." And the two of them raced down to the little cabin. As he landed on the deck, she was there, waiting for him. She stopped, looked at him, and said, "And this isn't just for the moment, is it?"

He looked at her in surprise, shook his head, and said, "Absolutely not. It's for every moment of every day that we enjoy being with each other." He added, "And I really hope it's forever."

She looked up, smiled, and said, "Remember. When you're young, it takes a lot of work, and, when you're older, you know what works."

"Sure," he said. "What do you mean though?"

She said, "It can be forever, if we want it to be."

"I want it to be," he said instantly. "You?"

"Oh, yeah," she said. She threw her arms around his neck and said, "Forever."

He lowered his head, and, just before their lips touched, he whispered right back, "Forever."

EPILOGUE

J ERRICHO CAME BACK from the fishing trip with a smile in his heart. He really had taken to fishing, like he hadn't ever expected. He would never be quite as addicted to the sport as was Greg, Eva's father, but Jerricho had gotten up every morning at five a.m. the past few days and couldn't wait to get on that lake. They had even tried afternoon fishing and evening fishing. The joy of catching that first fish had hooked Jerricho for life. He had promised to come back soon and often. And that was a promise that he would thoroughly enjoy keeping.

As it was, he headed back to what was his soulless apartment now. After being at the cabin, where the four of them were ensconced in Greg's environment and his joy in life, plus recuperating from exhaustion and the emotional impact of everything they'd been through, Jerricho found his apartment empty and without merit anymore.

He had never really cared before, but it was starting to really, just after this trip, get to him. As he sat here, out on his deck, a cold beer in his hand, his phone rang.

He looked down to see Diesel as the Caller ID. "Hey, Diesel," he said. "Did you catch any fish for me this morning?"

"Actually," he said, "I caught my first trout."

"Damn!" he said. "I'm so sad I had to leave."

"Did you have to leave though?" he asked. "Couldn't you have stayed?"

"Well, I still have to get my life together. You get to sit back and relax now. I'm not sure exactly what you'll do with your life or what she'll do with your life," he said, "but I just felt like it was time for me to leave."

"Well, what I'll do now is," he said, "is usher you into your next mission."

There was a moment's pause, then he said, "Seriously?"

"Yep, seriously."

"When?"

"Well you better finish that beer in your hand," he said in a dry tone.

"Shit! Are you watching me?"

"I wouldn't be so intrusive," he said, "but I have to tell you that's what I do too, when I hit home. I sit back on the deck, and I pull out a beer."

"Yeah, that's exactly what I'm doing. So what am I supposed to be doing, if I have to finish this beer?"

"You're heading out in less than three hours."

"Crap!" he said. "I haven't even done laundry."

"First thing you do after a mission," he said, "is you check out what you need to get done to leave again."

"I didn't have a chance yet. I've only been home a couple hours."

"You got enough clean clothes?"

"If I don't, you'll find them for me, won't you?"

"I absolutely will," he said.

"So where am I going?" he said.

"Switzerland," he said with a laugh. "You fly out very soon."

"Why?"

"Well, I'd tell you but, you know what? I don't want to ruin it for you."

"What'll ruin it for me?"

"Somebody you know is in trouble," he said. "It came through official channels, but, when I recognized the name, I figured you'd want to know."

"Who?" he asked, hopping to his feet. "Not too many people in my world I care about."

He said, "Yeah, I hear you there. And then I remembered the conversation we had with Eva."

At that, his stomach sank. "Jesus Christ," he said, "is it Brenna?"

"Yes, it is," Diesel said. "She was on a media trip. I didn't realize she was a journalist."

"I didn't either. And what happened?"

"She and her cameraman have been kidnapped. They were on a trip through Switzerland, heading toward Libya. Obviously they didn't make it. They have disappeared in the mountains."

"Ah, hell," he said. "Where's her husband?"

"Well, that's the thing," he said, "I don't have any record of a husband."

"Last I heard, she was getting married," he protested.

"Well, maybe you heard wrong, but she's over there, alone, except for the one cameraman with her."

"Any … any other intel?"

"I'll send it as soon as I get it," he said. "You need to get a move on now." And, with that, Diesel rang off.

Jerricho turned to look around at the small apartment, and, out loud, he said, "Well, I didn't like this place anyway."

He threw back the rest of his beer, quickly switched out

the dirty clothes in his duffel bag with a clean batch, and was out the door. As he made it to the front curb, he realized he didn't have a ride.

When a vehicle raced toward him, he laughed. "Damn, I like this job."

And, with that, he was gone.

This concludes Book 13 of The Mavericks: Diesel.
Read about Jerricho: The Mavericks, Book 14

Jerricho: Maverick (Book #14)

What happens when the very men—trained to make the hard decisions—come up against the rules and regulations that hold them back from doing what needs to be done? They either stay and work within the constraints given to them or they walk away. Only now, for a select few, they have another option:

The Mavericks. A covert black ops team that steps up and break all the rules … but gets the job done.

Welcome to a new military romance series by *USA Today* best-selling author Dale Mayer. A series where you meet new friends and just might get to meet old ones too in this raw and compelling look at the men who keep us safe every day from the darkness where they operate—and live—in the shadows … until someone special helps them step into the light.

Jerricho didn't expect his first solo mission to send him to the Middle East nor to rescue his journalist ex-wife and her cameraperson. Finding out why they and the other women had been taken was horrifying in itself, but saving a larger group than he'd first expected then complicates the rescue in a much bigger way.

Brenna had hopes that her ex would show up, as she knew the type of work he did. She'd always wanted a chance to show him how much she'd changed. This was hardly the ideal time, but she might not get a second chance.

Rescuing the women and taking out the kidnappers should have been the end of it, until they realize it's not as simple as it first seems. The women were objects initially; now they're targets …

Find book 14 here!

To find out more visit Dale Mayer's website.

https://geni.us/DMJerrichoUniversal

Author's Note

Thank you for reading Diesel: The Mavericks, Book 13! If you enjoyed the book, please take a moment and leave a short review.

Dear reader,

I love to hear from readers, and you can contact me at my website: www.dalemayer.com or at my Facebook author page. To be informed of new releases and special offers, sign up for my newsletter or follow me on BookBub. And if you are interested in joining Dale Mayer's Reader Group, here is the Facebook sign up page.
http://geni.us/DaleMayerFBGroup

Cheers,
Dale Mayer

About the Author

Dale Mayer is a *USA Today* best-selling author, best known for her SEALs military romances, her Psychic Visions series, and her Lovely Lethal Garden cozy series. Her contemporary romances are raw and full of passion and emotion (Broken But … Mending, Hathaway House series). Her thrillers will keep you guessing (Kate Morgan, By Death series), and her romantic comedies will keep you giggling (*It's a Dog's Life*, a stand-alone novella; and the Broken Protocols series, starring Charming Marvin, the cat).

Dale honors the stories that come to her—and some of them are crazy, break all the rules and cross multiple genres!

To go with her fiction, she also writes nonfiction in many different fields, with books available on résumé writing, companion gardening, and the US mortgage system. All her books are available in print and ebook format.

Connect with Dale Mayer Online

Dale's Website – www.dalemayer.com
Twitter – @DaleMayer
Facebook Page – geni.us/DaleMayerFBFanPage
Facebook Group – geni.us/DaleMayerFBGroup
BookBub – geni.us/DaleMayerBookbub
Instagram – geni.us/DaleMayerInstagram
Goodreads – geni.us/DaleMayerGoodreads
Newsletter – geni.us/DaleNews

Also by Dale Mayer

Published Adult Books:

Hathaway House

Aaron, Book 1

Brock, Book 2

Cole, Book 3

Denton, Book 4

Elliot, Book 5

Finn, Book 6

Gregory, Book 7

Heath, Book 8

Iain, Book 9

Jaden, Book 10

Keith, Book 11

Lance, Book 12

Melissa, Book 13

Nash, Book 14

Owen, Book 15

Hathaway House, Books 1–3

Hathaway House, Books 4–6

Hathaway House, Books 7–9

The K9 Files

Ethan, Book 1

Pierce, Book 2

Zane, Book 3

Lovely Lethal Gardens

Lovely Lethal Gardens, Books 3–4
Lovely Lethal Gardens, Books 5–6
Lovely Lethal Gardens, Books 7–8
Lovely Lethal Gardens, Books 9–10

Psychic Vision Series

Tuesday's Child
Hide 'n Go Seek
Maddy's Floor
Garden of Sorrow
Knock Knock…
Rare Find
Eyes to the Soul
Now You See Her
Shattered
Into the Abyss
Seeds of Malice
Eye of the Falcon
Itsy-Bitsy Spider
Unmasked
Deep Beneath
From the Ashes
Stroke of Death
Ice Maiden
Psychic Visions Books 1–3
Psychic Visions Books 4–6
Psychic Visions Books 7–9

By Death Series

Touched by Death
Haunted by Death
Chilled by Death
By Death Books 1–3

Broken Protocols – Romantic Comedy Series
Cat's Meow
Cat's Pajamas
Cat's Cradle
Cat's Claus
Broken Protocols 1-4

Broken and... Mending
Skin
Scars
Scales (of Justice)
Broken but... Mending 1-3

Glory
Genesis
Tori
Celeste
Glory Trilogy

Biker Blues
Morgan: Biker Blues, Volume 1
Cash: Biker Blues, Volume 2

SEALs of Honor
Mason: SEALs of Honor, Book 1
Hawk: SEALs of Honor, Book 2
Dane: SEALs of Honor, Book 3
Swede: SEALs of Honor, Book 4
Shadow: SEALs of Honor, Book 5
Cooper: SEALs of Honor, Book 6
Markus: SEALs of Honor, Book 7
Evan: SEALs of Honor, Book 8
Mason's Wish: SEALs of Honor, Book 9

Heroes for Hire

Logan's Light: Heroes for Hire, Book 6
Harrison's Heart: Heroes for Hire, Book 7
Saul's Sweetheart: Heroes for Hire, Book 8
Dakota's Delight: Heroes for Hire, Book 9
Michael's Mercy (Part of Sleeper SEAL Series)
Tyson's Treasure: Heroes for Hire, Book 10
Jace's Jewel: Heroes for Hire, Book 11
Rory's Rose: Heroes for Hire, Book 12
Brandon's Bliss: Heroes for Hire, Book 13
Liam's Lily: Heroes for Hire, Book 14
North's Nikki: Heroes for Hire, Book 15
Anders's Angel: Heroes for Hire, Book 16
Reyes's Raina: Heroes for Hire, Book 17
Dezi's Diamond: Heroes for Hire, Book 18
Vince's Vixen: Heroes for Hire, Book 19
Ice's Icing: Heroes for Hire, Book 20
Johan's Joy: Heroes for Hire, Book 21
Galen's Gemma: Heroes for Hire, Book 22
Zack's Zest: Heroes for Hire, Book 23
Bonaparte's Belle: Heroes for Hire, Book 24
Heroes for Hire, Books 1–3
Heroes for Hire, Books 4–6
Heroes for Hire, Books 7–9
Heroes for Hire, Books 10–12
Heroes for Hire, Books 13–15

SEALs of Steel

Badger: SEALs of Steel, Book 1
Erick: SEALs of Steel, Book 2
Cade: SEALs of Steel, Book 3
Talon: SEALs of Steel, Book 4
Laszlo: SEALs of Steel, Book 5

Geir: SEALs of Steel, Book 6
Jager: SEALs of Steel, Book 7
The Final Reveal: SEALs of Steel, Book 8
SEALs of Steel, Books 1–4
SEALs of Steel, Books 5–8
SEALs of Steel, Books 1–8

The Mavericks
Kerrick, Book 1
Griffin, Book 2
Jax, Book 3
Beau, Book 4
Asher, Book 5
Ryker, Book 6
Miles, Book 7
Nico, Book 8
Keane, Book 9
Lennox, Book 10
Gavin, Book 11
Shane, Book 12
Diesel, Book 13
Jerricho, Book 14
The Mavericks, Books 1–2
The Mavericks, Books 3–4
The Mavericks, Books 5–6
The Mavericks, Books 7–8
The Mavericks, Books 9–10
The Mavericks, Books 11–12

Bullard's Battle Series
Ryland's Reach, Book 1
Cain's Cross, Book 2
Eton's Escape, Book 3

Garret's Gambit, Book 4

Kano's Keep, Book 5

Fallon's Flaw, Book 6

Quinn's Quest, Book 7

Bullard's Beauty, Book 8

Collections

Dare to Be You…

Dare to Love…

Dare to be Strong…

RomanceX3

Standalone Novellas

It's a Dog's Life

Riana's Revenge

Second Chances

Published Young Adult Books:

Family Blood Ties Series

Vampire in Denial

Vampire in Distress

Vampire in Design

Vampire in Deceit

Vampire in Defiance

Vampire in Conflict

Vampire in Chaos

Vampire in Crisis

Vampire in Control

Vampire in Charge

Family Blood Ties Set 1–3

Family Blood Ties Set 1–5

Family Blood Ties Set 4–6

Family Blood Ties Set 7–9

Sian's Solution, A Family Blood Ties Series Prequel
    Novelette

Design series

Dangerous Designs

Deadly Designs

Darkest Designs

Design Series Trilogy

Standalone

In Cassie's Corner

Gem Stone (a Gemma Stone Mystery)

Time Thieves

Published Non-Fiction Books:

Career Essentials

Career Essentials: The Résumé

Career Essentials: The Cover Letter

Career Essentials: The Interview

Career Essentials: 3 in 1

www.ingramcontent.com/pod-product-compliance
Lightning Source LLC
Chambersburg PA
CBHW070527100726
47907CB00004B/1014